"*An Army of Lovers* explores the liminal spaces where cities and individuals come together and stand apart with strange, brainy grace." — Michelle Tea, author of *Mermaid in Chelsea Creek*

"Too often in the poetry world, self-awareness means dreary, self-important self-absorption. Thank goodness that is not the case here. This picaresque story about the 'particular lostness' of poetry, the ways poems always win and the lives of self-described 'mediocre' poets is actually pretty hilarious! It's also smart, incisive and politically astute. Now, to the barricades!" — Rebecca Brown, author of *American Romances: Essays*

"Two of my favorite poets, each with a unique voice, wangle a 'third mind' as they come together in a novel radically different than any I know. Like the 70s Rosa von Praunheim documentary on the 2nd wave gay rights movement (*Army of Lovers or The Revolt of the Perverts*), the newly minted *Army of Lovers* takes a stage crowded with multiple images, intent on creating a moment of revolutionary stillness inside the noise. Authors Spahr and Buuck, who appear in this novel as Bay Area poets 'Koki' and 'Demented Panda,' style it up all the way from magical realism to 'new journalism' and Raymond Carver Cathedralspeak, but it's the weary 'I can't go on. I'll go on' optimism at which wounded veterans of the army of lovers excel. Theirs is a rigorous book, and a book of marvels, with something funny, something painful, stirring on every page." — Kevin Killian, author of *Spreadeagle*

AN ARMY
OF LOVERS

AN ARMY
OF LOVERS

Juliana Spahr and David Buuck

City Lights | San Francisco

Library of Congress Cataloging-in-Publication Data
Spahr, Juliana.
An army of lovers / Juliana Spahr and David Buuck.
    pages cm
ISBN 978-0-87286-629-4 (pbk.)
1. Poets—Fiction. 2. Political fiction. 3. Experimental fiction. I. Buuck,
David. II. Title.

PS3569.P3356
[A76 2013]
813'.54—dc23

2013020598

City Lights Books are published at the City Lights Bookstore,
261 Columbus Avenue, San Francisco, CA 94133.
www.citylights.com

CONTENTS

The blood on George Bush's
Hands keeps coming out in my stool.
Night is never dark enough because
Everything I see frightens me.

—Charles Bernstein,
"The Sixties, with Apologies"

We work too hard.
We're too tired
to fall in love.
Therefore we must
overthrow the government.

We work too hard.
We're too tired
to overthrow the government.
Therefore we must
fall in love.

—Rod Smith, *Pour le CGT*

A PICTURESQUE STORY ABOUT
THE BORDER BETWEEN TWO CITIES

THE SAN FRANCISCO BAY AREA can boast of having both many great poets and many mediocre poets. Among the mediocre were two poets better known as Demented Panda and Koki. These two poets thought of themselves as living life in pursuit of both the intellectual and the social pleasures of poetry. In this they were like most people who considered themselves poets.

It is important to realize that in the time of Demented Panda and Koki poetry was an art form that had lost most, if not all, of its reasons for being. It was no longer considered, because of its ties to song, the superior way for a culture to remember something about itself. And at the same time, it was also no longer considered the superior way for a nation to inspire patriotism and proclaim, with elaborate rhyme and rhythm, that its values were great and universal values. This was especially true in the nation that claimed Demented Panda and Koki among its citizens. This nation had long ago realized that the best way to inspire patriotism and convince other nations that its values were great and universal was to offer a series of tax breaks and incentives that encouraged the international distribution of colorful moving pictures and songs that celebrated soldiers, government agents, and upwardly mobile consumers as heroes.

It was in part precisely because poetry had lost its patriotic importance that Demented Panda and Koki were so devoted to it. But as poetry had lost its patriotic importance, it had also lost much, if not all, of its potential to be a meaningful part of any sort of resistance movement. It was not as if they had totally given up. They knew that poetry still had a role in various anti-colonial movements in cultures other than theirs. But they found it impossible to imagine any equivalent role in their own culture today. Despite this lack of faith in their ability to be meaningful poets, they remained devoted to poetry, full of hope about its possibilities, no matter how limited these seemed to be. As they remained devoted to poetry, they met frequently to take long walks together, and on these walks they talked about poetry and its particular lostness.

When they walked, they took up a lot of room

on the sidewalk. Demented Panda usually brought his two dogs, who tended to yip and yap at other dogs and at skateboarders, and Koki frequently pushed her baby in a stroller. Demented Panda and Koki thus walked down the street with three other sentient beings in tow, sometimes talking loudly like the baby, laughing and enjoying the sun, which was often accompanied by a cool breeze, and sometimes, like the dogs, getting in each other's way and then being annoyed and snippy with each other or with the world at large.

During these walks, what they would talk about could probably be best described as gossip, although it was also about poems and poetry. They didn't gossip about poets or poetry they didn't like. So they didn't talk much about poetry that tends to portray, in a quiet and overly serious tone, with a studied and crafted attention to line breaks for emphasis and a moving epiphany or denouement at the end, the deep thoughts held by individuals in a consumerist society. Instead, they talked about poetry that they liked, the sort that stretches language to reveal its potential for ambiguity, fragmentation, and self-assertion within chaos, the sort that uses open forms and cross-cultural content, the sort that appropriates images from popular culture and the media and refashions them, even if they often also talked about their frustrations with and the limitations of these kinds of poetries that they nonetheless liked.

During their walks they often played a sort of game where one of them would say something negative about some poem and then the other would say something positive and then one of them would say something negative and this would go on and on for some time. They were fairly ecumenical in their approach. They talked in negatives and positives about their own work and each other's work and the work of others. It was a sort of erotics to them, this moving of their brains between saying something negative and then something positive. It was like a game of one-upmanship that they played with each other and with the poems themselves. Some days Demented Panda was more negative and Koki more positive. But other days Koki was more negative and Demented Panda more positive. But when it came down to it, at the end of the flipping back and forth, the poems always won, and if they made a list of work that they liked, their lists would probably be remarkably similar and it would be that work that they talked about together, no matter how much they complained about the poems or gossiped about the poets while walking on any given afternoon.

One summer day, a particularly nice and mostly sunny day of 69 degrees, while on one of their many walks, Demented Panda and Koki decided to collaborate. They would, they said to themselves, write something that they would come to call *A Picturesque Story About the Border Between Two Cities.* Demented Panda and Koki lived only 1.4 miles from one another but they lived in different cities. They said to themselves that in *A Picturesque Story About the Border Between Two Cities* they would write something about what it meant to be poets in this time, this time of wars and economic inequality and environmental collapse, and in this particular urban space, a place that put up signs claiming to be a "Nuclear Free Zone" despite being the place that was largely responsible for the development of the nuclear bomb, a place that was now defined by the development of a technology industry that distributed colorful moving pictures and songs and social media through flatscreens of various sizes. They hoped that if they thought hard enough, they might be able to figure out some possible new configurations for political art and action. They wanted to think about the connections among place and time and writing as more than just an artistic problem, and also about how a site can be a complex cipher of the unstable relationships that define the present crises and their living within them.

But mainly they tended to say to themselves what they did not want to do. They did not want to write something that did what they already tended to do, something that was all clever about capitalism or all pious with long lists of endangered plants and animals and statistics that made you feel sad or all celebratory of poets and friendship or all self-lacerating or self-flagellating or self-cancelling or all about their edgy sexuality or all deep and serious with dramatic line breaks and well-crafted prosody or all jokey and deliberately bad and all about the genre or all full of found language edited to be either serious or funny. They did not, in other words, leave themselves a lot of possible things to do. As a result, their collaboration was more about what they did not want to do than what they wanted to do, even as their hope was that through the collaboration they might figure out what it meant to be a poet in a time and a culture where poetry had lost most if not all of its reasons for being, might by telling their picturesque story about a border between two cities find a new elsewhere, whether in poetry or as poets.

To begin this project, Demented Panda and Koki did not choose an obvious part of the border between the two cities, such as the intersection where people had once marched against the Vietnam war from Koki's city to Demented Panda's city and at the border had met the police and a motorcycle gang from Demented Panda's city and a brawl had ensued, even though this brawl more or less summed up the mythic histories that their two cities told about themselves, one claiming to be lefty and the other claiming to be bad-ass. Instead, after much wrangling and many misfires they decided to locate their picturesque story on a plot of land that was more or less equidistant from each of their houses and that included the border between their two cities. It was hard to say what exactly the plot of land was. It was small, about .27 miles around its perimeter. They could tell from looking at it that it was flat, somewhat rectangular in shape, with the distended sides of the rectangle going north-south. But the plot was not really a rectangle in any meaningful way as it had a hump on the northeast side and came to a point on the southernmost tip. A heavy-rail public rapid transit system emerged from an underground tunnel in the middle of the plot and traversed the north-south axis of the rectangle on an elevated platform. When the trains headed through Koki's city they travelled beneath it, entering and exiting through the plot of land at the border between their cities. When the trains travelled through Demented Panda's city they travelled above it on raised rails and towering concrete hubs. On the southwestern corner of the plot, three streets and ten lanes of traffic met, regulated by three stoplights and numerous security cameras. A sidewalk was available for pedestrian access and there were benches every so often along the sidewalk. The rotting wood of the benches had been recently painted by children and featured self-improvement slogans such as "drink 8 glasses of water a day." There were also two metal sculptures facing each other across the border between the two cities that spelled out the words "HERE" and "THERE." "HERE" was north of "THERE" and read north to east, while "THERE" read south to east. The sculpture was a kind of joke for those who knew about poetry or who knew about the Bay Area, but it was not much of a joke and certainly didn't make the plot of land any more poetic to the two mediocre Bay Area poets.

In order to collaborate on the writing of *A Picturesque Story About the Border Between Two Cities*, Demented Panda and Koki met several times a week that summer on the small plot of land. There they sat and talked in the partly cloudy 78 degrees or in the sunny 77 degrees or in the sunny 76 degrees, the dogs panting at their feet, the baby cooing with pleasure at each passing truck. Those passing by might have mistaken them for sunbathers or picnickers enjoying a summer's respite from the hard labor of toiling in the intellectual mines of the academy, but Demented Panda and Koki had only one thing on their mind and it was the small plot of land. It is true that their conversations frequently turned to urban theory, site-specific performance, environmental art, and debates concerning gentrification and public space, but at the same time, they tried to focus all such wide-ranging conversations, with their detours into gossip and doubt, back onto the small plot of land, the plot for their picturesque story about the border between two cities. And as they did this, they talked frequently and repeatedly about how despite the amount of research they had done they were increasingly not that interested in the small plot of land. And then they would talk about how it made them feel uncomfortable to be there on the small plot of land attempting to write about it when they were not interested in it and how also they had no clear right to write about it because of who they were, although they always left who they were unspecified. And they talked about how they did not want to present the small plot of land as un-inhabited because they imagined that certain people lived and slept on the small plot of land. They talked a lot about how they didn't want to bother these people but they didn't want to ignore them either and about the ethical issues around this sort of neighbor-love and its representation in poetry. But as they spent more time on the small plot of land they began to realize that very few bothered to live or sleep on the small plot of land. The small plot of land was probably both too isolated and too exposed. Plus, beginning early each morning, it was regularly blasted with the vibrations and clamor of the heavy-rail public rapid transit system trains thrusting into or out of the ground as they moved people to and from either city. The people that they imagined lived and slept on the small plot of land and that they talked about not wanting to bother mostly only passed by the small plot of land, despite its many park benches, on their way to slightly more accommodating plots of land, like the street corner where Koki lived, which had hedges for privacy, or the abandoned lot with the burned-down house on the street where Demented Panda lived.

In setting their proposed picturesque story on the small plot of land, Demented Panda and Koki were somewhat right that nothing much dramatic had happened there. Even the story of the heavy-rail public rapid transit system that passed through it, a story that in the city of Demented Panda was accompanied by the razing of vibrant, multiethnic working-class communities, had not been that dramatically controversial as it had merely replaced an already existing railroad line that had been in place since the turn of the century.

Yet looked at another way, the plot of land had all the histories of the surrounding areas, some of them sad, some of them triumphant. It had for many, many years been populated by various humans and animals, such as rabbits and other small rodents, large deer, elk, and antelope, and various birds, some migratory and some not. The humans hunted these animals and they burned the grasslands regularly and they harvested roots and tubers that they planted. They call themselves various names and spoke various languages. This history Demented Panda and Koki did not know all that well and was only vaguely told in their time. But the history that came after they knew fairly well. In the quick telling of this history, despite the humans who had for three thousand years been hunting the animals and burning the grasslands and planting and harvesting the roots and tubers, the land had been considered unclaimed and unpopulated by an expedition of people sent by that other nation far away who then claimed it for another nation and then a representative of that nation gave the land that included the small plot of land to a member of one such expedition. From then on, different nations and many different people claimed the land. There were many lawsuits. A couple of armed skirmishes. And various deals were made and continued to be made. The land was now claimed by an entirely different nation from the one that sent the expedition and was owned by many different people, as long as they defined ownership in the same way the nation who now occupied the land did.

As they began their collaboration, they talked about the fickle nature of observation, about how they would walk to the small plot of land not really noticing anything but then once they got there they would perk up and begin to put on their "picturesque story" mindset and then look around for things to write about. They wondered if they should go through life using the "picturesque story" mindset all the time or if they should refuse the "picturesque story" mindset when they were at the small plot of land or if it was okay to use it some of the time and not other times. They did not even know what to call the small plot of land that they had settled on for their picturesque story. They agreed that it was not a park, despite the presence of park benches and trees and grass. It was certainly never used as a park because it was surrounded by large amounts of traffic and every few minutes the heavy-rail public rapid transit trains careened through. But they were also hesitant to call it a median strip because it was a bit wider than most median strips and had the kind of public art one wouldn't see on a median strip. And so they kept on referring to it as the small plot of land.

When it came to the writing of poetry, Demented Panda and Koki were badly matched. Their mismatchedness could be seen in the accoutrements that they used in their writing lives. Demented Panda always carried a notebook, but a notebook that might be called the littlest of notebooks. He kept this notebook in the front pocket of whatever jacket he was wearing on any given afternoon and it was so small that there was never an unsightly bulge. He carried a notebook at all times because he was a poet but he carried a littlest notebook because he didn't want to have to commit to writing anything really and the littleness of the notebook made it difficult to really write anything even if he had wanted to. Koki, on the other hand, carried with her at all times a backpack. In this backpack, she kept no fewer than five identical pens lined up for easy access in the pen holder section.

And in the backpack itself she always kept at least one large and thick notebook and a book for reading in case she was stuck for some reason somewhere for a long period of time with nothing much to do, along with the usual detritus of modern female life, like lip balms and tampons and small tins of painkillers.

As they talked about the small plot of land they also, of course, talked about themselves. They talked about how their writing might sometimes do a kind of political work but still leave them dissatisfied. And they talked about their own tendency to write things so as to show themselves and others that they had the right attitudes about various things. They talked about failure and shame and about maybe making failure and shame the work, how maybe this talking of theirs was a kind of doing even if it was mostly doing nothing and, like poetry, seemed to make nothing happen. They talked about collaborating and how the personal and the political and bodies and sex and work and wanting and writing and writhing can get all fucked up, can get in the way, even if they could not exactly say what it was in the way of. They talked a lot about their bodies, their bodily aches and pains, their signs of infection, their nipple discharge and breast swelling, their bizarre behavior, agitations, hallucinations, and depersonalizations, their severe dizziness and drowsiness and confusion, how all these might be part of their collaboration as well, part of the picturesque story they might tell about living as a poet today, a story about that complex cipher of unstable relationships that define life under capitalism.

When they talked, Demented Panda usually said things in the negative and Koki usually took notes. After all this talking, Koki would then make the face, the not-quite-exasperated-yet-thinking-hard-about-it-but-also-frustrated face. And when Koki made the face Demented Panda usually made a joke or he would propose that the way beyond their impasses and their symptoms and side effects would be to create a giant mess. Demented Panda liked to talk about what he called the dialectics of mess, how he would hold his messes back or would hold his messes in his back where they could make pain instead of progress. He would talk about the messes he was maybe going to make, or talk about the messes he had already made but weren't quite done somehow, or about how his back hurt from holding all his messiness there, or about his never-finished messertation, which he thought maybe was no longer a good or a relevant mess, or about his messuscripts that he also thought were no longer good or relevant messes. And then when he would get frustrated or bored with the mess coming out of his mouth, Demented Panda would turn and talk to his dogs in a voice that mocked itself in direct proportion to its seeming earnestness, as if the dogs could only understand philosophical questions or aesthetic questions or political questions if rendered in a cartoon voice.

In moments like these, Koki would again make the face, the not-quite-exasperated-yet-thinking-hard-about-it-but-also-frustrated face. She would stop taking notes, put down her pen, and tell Demented Panda to stop with the jokes. She would say that it was making her insane, not the jokes but the not finishing *A Picturesque Story About the Border Between Two Cities*, and if he wasn't going to do something productive for the collaboration with his small notebooks, then at least he could let her get some work done. And then it again would be Demented Panda's turn to make the face, the not-quite-exasperated-yet-thinking-hard-about-it-but-also-frustrated face. And then one or both of them would call to the baby or the dogs, in a chirpy bird-brained voice or a dopey cartoon bear voice or maybe make faces at the baby or rub the dogs behind the ears and the baby would perk up and giggle and the dogs would turn and push their hind-flanks into the poets, while sniffing at the small plot of land, and then Demented Panda and Koki would get back to their talking and their note-taking and their exasperations and their frustrations and the hard work of unproductive labor.

So this is how they spent their summer, talking about themselves as they talked about the small plot of land, and the more they talked about the small plot of land and themselves at the same time the more they began to consider this talking their art practice, an art practice of meeting and, while there, doing some talking instead of doing some doing.

The days wore on. It was a sunny 78 degrees one day and then a partly cloudy 77 degrees the next and then a more sunny 79 degrees the day after that and then a slightly sunny 76 degrees followed by a mostly sunny 75 degrees. Then suddenly the summer was over. And they realized they both had worked all summer on *A Picturesque Story About the Border Between Two Cites* and they had both written the same amount, which was more or less nothing. It is true that by the end of the summer Demented Panda had some notes in his notebook that he kept promising to type up and send to Koki along with some audio recordings he had made while walking around the small plot of land at night, but he never did. And it is true that Koki had written pages and pages, and then rewritten those pages and pages night after night, but her pages were so wandering and incomprehensible that they were the same as nothing.

Nonetheless, Demented Panda and Koki agreed to meet one last time on the small plot of land and talk one more time about *A Picturesque Story About the Border Between Two Cities*. Demented Panda decided for this last meeting that he wanted to make a right proper big final mess. He decided he was going to cast a spell and then he mumbled something about how the first poems were probably spells. Koki then mumbled to herself that of course Demented Panda would choose a spell because spells are short and fit without effort into small notebooks and do nothing but nonetheless she eagerly agreed to be a witness to it. So this time Koki left the baby with its father and Demented Panda left the dogs in his house with a couple of rawhide bones to keep them occupied and, in the mostly sunny 76 degrees, they walked one more time to the small plot of land and there met for what they hoped would be one last time, one last mess.

Demented Panda's spell was a simple one, aimed at gathering energy from the plot of land and its environs and from such energies shaping their picturesque story into poetry. And Demented Panda thought to himself that because the place didn't have much energy, as it just had a lot of commuters traveling by car or rail around and through and beneath it, when the spell did not work, it would of course make perfect sense. He could then add it to his list of unfinished messes and write about that in the littlest notebook that he kept in the front pocket of his jacket.

To begin his spell, Demented Panda sat down and crossed his legs and then adjusted his stomach over his lap and then reached down and pulled his ballsack forward so he could really clear his mind and become one with himself. After he cleared his mind, he cleared his mind again. He felt that he really needed a clear mind to make the spell work, or as he figured it, not work. Then he held out two of his arms or legs and made his paws into fists. He then felt some sort of energy, perhaps the energy of the entire universe as the spell's instructions had promised, enter his recessive paw and flow up from his ballsack and through his body and into his projective paw. He let the energy build up in his projective paw until he felt he had an immense amount of it. Then he flung his paws to the right, opened his projective paw and, while doing this, he envisioned the energies flying outward. He then recited a quick chant, one that went "give orange give me eat orange me eat orange give me eat orange give me you," a chant that was something Nim Chimpsky, the famous chimp who had been taught sign language by his human caretakers, had liked to sign when he was hungry for an orange. Demented Panda had decided to use the mumbling signs of Nim Chimpsky as a chant because they were slightly absurd and slightly meaningless, and reeked a little of dubious science, all of which seemed the perfect combination for his goal of performance art, the kind of performance art that someone like Demented Panda might turn to so as to express the complete collapse and failure of a project, not so much as a last resort but as the right proper culmination of the lostness of a summer and the lostness of poetry and the lostness of being a mediocre Bay Area poet.

Despite Demented Panda's skepticism and his desire for picturesque performance art, the spell worked, in a certain sense of the word, and though what happened next began rather mundanely, it can best be described not with poetry but by resorting to the language Tommy Lee used in his description of the party that Pamela Anderson threw for his thirty-third birthday, along with various first-person accounts of the Woodstock concert of 1999, and Livy's description of the Bacchanalia in his *History of Rome*. What happened next began with shit. Raw sewage began pouring out of the heavy-rail public rapid transit system tunnel and collecting in a series of small pools or lakes on the small plot of land. At first, Demented Panda and Koki just sat there as if slightly stoned from the shock of the spell working and watched the pool of sewage seeping up and out of the small plot of land. The flood of sewage grew to be fifty feet long and perhaps a foot deep and soon it flowed over the laps of Demented Panda and Koki and into the intersection, where cars continued driving through it.

The smell of the raw sewage seemed to only intensify Demented Panda's spell-casting, mess-making desires, so he got up from his seated position and stood in the middle of the small plot of land whirring his arms over his head as if signaling to an invisible fleet of helicopters that it was time to land, and as a result of this whirring, two rows of flames appeared, stretching out for hundreds of feet in front of him and then, just as suddenly, young girls in sheer flowing gowns and bare feet appeared all around him and sang "give orange give me eat orange me eat orange give me eat orange give me you" over and over as they unrolled a red carpet between the lines of fire. Clowns and acrobats materialized, filling the air with confetti. A giant on stilts dressed as the devil walked through the tangle of girls, parting them like a sea. There was a Ferris wheel, roller coasters, contortionists in boxes, caged lions, and bubble machines. Impertinent beings in white face and breasty girls in top hats then began to practice debaucheries of every kind, as each found at hand the form of consumption to which he or she was disposed by the passion predominant in his or her nature, such as the pushing out of butts from the wearing of high heels or the accenting of the genitalia with tight pants or the excessive ornamentation and exaggeration of secondary sexual characteristics or the promiscuous intercourse of eating high levels of refined sugar, white flour, trans fat, polyunsaturated fats, and salt, or the burning of excessive amounts of fossil fuels by endlessly idling buses and trucks. Koki looked around and she noticed diamond-covered push-up bras, pubic areas vajazzled with Swarovski crystal ornaments instead of hair, skyscraper heels covered with pavé-style tiny twinkling crystals, and diamond-encrusted dog tags. Demented Panda looked around and he noticed stands filled with hawkers of food, such as Dove Bars, Frozen Lemonades, Iced Mochas, Orange Mango Drinks, Sprites, Pepsis, Cokes, Nachos, Tenders and Poppers, Jelly Buns, Fat-Free Soft Serve

Ice Creams, Gourmet Butter Salt Potatoes, Caramel Apples, Jelly Bellys, Doughnuts, and Arepas. Enormous mounted speakers amplified angry and ecstatic guitar solos, trap drums playing taps, and brass trumpets playing reveille. Musicians kept appearing and joining in, some blowing their horns from great distances, others using joysticks or satellite communication systems to control their computers and samplers and sound processors and circuit-bent video game consoles. DJs spun and scratched the dented hubcaps of half-exploded armed personnel carriers, the hillbilly armor attached to sprawling networks of scrapped wiring and repurposed military hardware, improvised exclamatory devices screeching into the general din and frenzy.

It was a big production, with a budget of $1,229,735,801,934.00. Camouflage-costumed figures rappelled from copters hovering above as others raised their arms to receive and pass along any number of bodies leaping and falling from above through pulsing strobe lights meant to induce sleep-deprivation, bewilderment, and increased motivations for compliance. The approximately 919,967 revelers lined up in a seemingly endless chorus line, arms linked or amputated stumps pressed up against one another, all singing in a half-whisper, "give orange give me eat orange me eat orange give me eat orange give me you." The musicians made sounds like Doppler-ized armored vehicles speeding by a riot at a heavy metal concert, with yelling and whistling and catcalls in what seemed like a hundred different languages, a riotous wash of voices shouting in the mosh pit, running, diving into the shit, with break-off factions scaling the twelve-foot-high, three-foot-thick rein-forced concrete Bremer walls that surrounded the entrance to the heavy-rail public rapid transit system, posing for the closed-circuit security cameras busy scanning the theater of operations in order to docu-ment all that's done in our name, before stage-diving into soft, greasy piles of Styrofoam nacho contain-ers, paper hamburger wrappers, cardboard french fry boxes, and plastic beer cups.

All of this was surrounded by mobile production trucks and, in the shadows behind the mobile pro-duction trucks, empty buses parked in double rows stretching out for at least a quarter of a mile, and in the darkness behind the buses, oversize tractor-trail-er trucks, the kind that transport forklifts and boilers and other heavy industrial equipment on superhigh-ways at night. All of these vehicles had brought all the excesses to the small plot of land and had their air conditioners and refrigeration units running, so they gurgled as they idled, spewing fumes until soon the small plot of land was covered with a dense brownish-yellow hazy cloud filled with the oxides of nitrogen and hydrocarbons.

Demented Panda and Koki wandered through the small plot of land. Except it was no longer only a small plot of land, but also an enormous food court. Except it wasn't just a food court, but also an outdoor rehearsal space lent to artists by a small nonprofit arts organization. Except it wasn't a rehearsal space, but a soundstage for gigantic live entertainments. Except it wasn't a soundstage, but a fake Baghdadi neighborhood staged for counterinsurgency training exercises. Not a fake neighborhood but an intersection in the Financial District on the night of March 23, 2003. Not an intersection but an interrogation room. Not an interrogation room but a holding cell funded by the Department of Homeland Security for counterterrorist efforts, holding 2,438 protestors in a nearby warehouse rented for this very purpose. Not a warehouse-turned-holding cell but a warehouse-turned-club where the after-party takes place. Not an after-party but an academic conference on politics and aesthetics. Not a conference but a boardroom meeting on tax-deductible philanthropic donations to nonprofit arts organizations.

Not a boardroom but a bunker, dug into the wet and muddy ground. Not a bunker but a book, each line redacted except for the numbers. Not a book but a bonfire made from its burning pages, with untold revelers dancing around it. Not a bonfire but a set of bright stage lights, illuminating the small plot of land so that the audience could better see the action. Except that there's no audience, since all this was happening now and everyone was knee-deep in it, not just watching but as embedded participants. Even pointing and gaping was participation. Even taking cellphone photos for documentation was participation. Even standing perfectly still and doing nothing was participation.

But Demented Panda and Koki did not bother to stand perfectly still, did not limit themselves to cellphone photographs or taking notes for their collaborative poem. Instead they muddled their way through the lakes of raw sewage that were slowly filling with empty pizza boxes and crushed Sprite bottles, and were both thrilled and anxious, excited by the unleashed energy and skeptical of its implications, eager to join in because the scenes they watched were part of a larger story of their time, which in turn was a very minor episode in the history of debauchery and excess in civilization. And these excesses were not confined to one species of vice, for from this storehouse of villainy also proceeded punching, slapping, and kicking, jumping on naked feet, breaking of jaws and teeth, arranging bodies in various sexually explicit positions for photographing, forcing groups to masturbate while being videotaped, searching of anal and vaginal cavities, placing dog chains or straps around necks and having others pose as if taking them for a walk, dragging off screaming into dark, dank places, handcuffing wrists high up on the back, injecting various unknown drugs without consent, using dogs without muzzles to intimidate and frighten, allowing dogs to bite and severely injure, masking and then abducting on small privately owned jets, drawing of blood samples, plugging of ears, placing of rags over faces and pouring water over them, cutting away of clothes with knives and scissors, breaking of chemical lights and pouring of phosphoric liquid on bodies, threatening with cocked 9mm pistols, pouring of cold water over bodies, beating with broom handles and chairs, threatening with rape, sodomizing with chemical lights and broom sticks, threatening with guns and power drills, forcing into dark boxes for extended periods of time, slamming of heads against walls, slapping of faces and abdomens, and holding open of eyes while shining a torch into them. Meanwhile, the sounds of the churning roller coasters, the mobile production trucks and the gurgling of their refrigeration units, and the arena rock anthems all served to conceal the swiping of debit cards and tapping of personal identification numbers, the cash registers ca-chinging, the barking and the breaking, the whimpering, the crying, the screaming.

At first, while all of this went on, Demented Panda and Koki joined in, running in circles and thrusting their hips forward and back, spinning their paws and claws around each other, thrusting their thumbs up and over their shoulders, making airborne chest-to-chest collisions while air-stroking their cocks, stopping now and then to pantomime a series of heretofore classified but since wikileaked enhanced interrogation techniques, contorting their mouths into idiotic grins. But eventually, after eating his fill of doughnuts and arepas, Demented Panda, bereft of reason and unable to enjoy the performance any longer, began to utter complaints, with frantic contortions of his body, mumbling over and over to himself that all he had wanted to do was write nothing about an unremarkable place, write a picturesque story of a post-pastoral plot of land. His frantic contortions now hovered somewhere between the panic-tremors of bodily shock and some kind of ecstatic postmodern dance.

Koki abruptly stopped and stood still and was silent for a long time, looking around and making the face, the not-quite-exasperated-yet-thinking-hard-about-it-but-also-frustrated face. And then she looked down at her hands. Koki's hands were normally fuzzy with down and sharp black talons, but one of them had now mutated into a pink and fleshy handgun, oozing and dripping amniotic fluid. Koki knew this dripping flesh handgun of hers well, for her hand oozed and dripped with amniotic fluid whenever for some absurd reason she thought she was not a part of what was going on around her. Koki thus suddenly knew her role and, in the habit of Bacchantes, with her hair disheveled, her claw now a flesh-gun dripping and oozing amniotic fluid, went to the mouth of the tunnel of the heavy-rail public rapid transit system and began shooting from her flesh-gun hand an inextinguishable flame composed of native sulphur and charcoal. As she did this Demented Panda followed along behind her plaintively asking her what she wanted and she looked at him for a moment and then shrugged, as if the answer should be obvious to anyone who had spent the summer visiting a small plot of land in an attempt to write *A Picturesque Story*

About the Border Between Two Cities. I want to burn it down, Koki said. And Demented Panda found it hard to argue with that and so stood beside her, his fur matted and covered with shit, feverishly rubbing his face as if trying to wipe the idiotic grin off his face, his eyes alight with the simple anticipatory pleasure of throwing more wood onto the fire.

Everything burned. And when everything had burned and all that was left was smoldering ashes, the spell ended. The mobile production trucks, the buses, the oversize tractor-trailer trucks, the careening ambulances all vanished, the musicians, the breasty girls in top hats, the food hawkers, the clowns and acrobats all vanished, but the raw sewage remained. With nothing holding them together, Demented Panda and Koki sat there in the raw sewage. All that was left was the feeling of sitting in raw sewage and knowing lostness deep inside.

There is an analogy, although far from perfect, that may shed some light on what went on that day. Imagine Edible Fig. Edible Fig was first domesticated outside his native region in Mesopotamia in the valley of the Tigris and Euphrates rivers, in what is today Iraq, and then he travelled to what is now California beginning in 1769. It is not clear to Edible Fig, nor to anyone else, how Edible Fig spreads into preserves and wild areas, but he does, and then once there he grows quickly and spreads vegetatively by root sprouts, forming dense thickets that exclude most other plants. This story is not just the easy and obvious one of invasion from afar. There are other ways that this analogy works. Most figs are dependent on a species-specific agaonid wasp and Edible Fig is no exception. And so, one afternoon, Fertilized Female Wasp squeezed through the scale-covered ostiole in the end of the syconia of caprifigs of Edible Fig and laid one egg in each of the short-style female flowers that Edible Fig was growing. Eventually, still inside the syconium, Adult Male Wasp emerged and quickly cut into the flower containing Female Wasp Larvae and mated with her. Female Wasp then gnawed her way out of the syconium two or three weeks after this and then she searched for another, younger syconium and squeezed through that narrow opening to reach the flowers inside. This opening was so small that some of the pollen on the body surface of Female Wasp was scraped off as she passed through. There she inserted her ovipositor down the style tube to deposit her eggs, but the styles of Edible Fig were so long that Female Wasp could not easily deposit her eggs, so she had to insert her ovipositor down the style tube again and again and as she attempted this again and again she deposited pollen and fertilized the flowers vigorously even though she realized that she would never be able to leave the syconium.

THE SIDE EFFECT

SHE HAD DONE WHAT she usually did. Upon arrival at her office, she turned on all her machines, the lights and the computer and the recording devices and the printer, and then proceeded to go through the new stack of forms, along with the student papers, the administrative emails, the healthcare forms, the websites, blogs, status updates, voicemails, the photos and videos. As she did this she ran her left hand along her thighs, and then under her blouse, over her breasts and down her side, until she felt it. A brown-black tick, burrowed into her flesh.

She got up, carefully pulled it out with a set of tweezers, taking it to the toilet to flush it and then wash her hands. She then turned to the Internet for advice or augury that presented itself as advice. The Internet said that if the tick had only been attached a short amount of time, then one wouldn't get sick, but the Internet also warned that one got sick when the tick vomited into the bloodstream, which is what the tick did when it first attached. The Internet said to get tested, but the Internet also warned of false negatives, of insurance companies denying coverage, of endless forms and requests and letters. The Internet also suggested various alternative remedies and treatments. It said ticks were full not only of anaplasmosis, babesiosis, ehrlichiosis, and Lyme disease but also full of the militarized mycoplasma fermentans incognitus, the result of Nazi experiments that had been relocated after the war to an island off the coast of Lyme, Connecticut. It said that the infections could be spread not just by ticks but also by humans through breastmilk, and although it denied it could be spread by other fluids such as semen or vaginal secretions or saliva, it noted that if two mice of the same gender, one infected and one not, were put in a cage, then both mice ended up infected.

Meanwhile, she continued to work. She filled out forms, signed them, put them in the manila envelope and exchanged them for another manila envelope full of more forms. She graded papers and signed the add/drop forms. She checked her email and her email checked her. She logged into various social networks and got updated. She downloaded information for work and worked on the information. She sat down in front of her machines and tried to work on her new composition. All the while checking her side for any evidence of a bull's-eye around the tick bite, as the Internet suggested she do.

She had her recording equipment spread out on her desk among the many piles and had several windows open on the computer screen. She had been trying to make a sound piece using found materials, a piece that might take all that she could know and feel about a military prison in another country and the bodies inside it, their movements and actions and sounds, and then somehow shape this into music, or protest, or she did not know what. Unlike her previous compositions, this project used sounds from the Internet that did not provide her with obvious notes or chords or melodies to represent what she was seeing and reading and feeling. She squirmed in her seat with a side-to-side motion while she focused on the search-engineered sounds and images the Internet delivered to her, trying to imagine the invisible sound waves emanating from each image's back glow, each soldier's frozen laugh, each detainee's duct-tape-covered mouth.

Her compositions tended to be melodic and rich. She usually made music about things like crows, not just any crow but the last remaining 'alalā, the Hawaiian crow that carried the souls of the dead to the underworld and that was now kept in a breeding cage because it was extinct in the wild. Or about a drop of water, a specific drop of water, such as a drop of water being fought over by multinational companies and an armed resistance movement in Cochabamba in 1990. She thought of music as a respite from representation, but she still tried to make her music feel like what she thought it felt like to think the thoughts she thought and feel the feelings she felt about the 'alalā or that last drop of Cochabamban water. She might begin with a dense chord that she would let reverberate in phrygian or lydian or dorian or locrian or aeolian modes, whatever she felt best represented the 'alalā or the drop of water in Cochabamba. She would then listen to the reverberations from each tone and from each chord and have some feelings that would lead her onward into the composition. The compositions were spare and lyrical. They were full of lament and loss.

But that day, she felt like the circuitry of all her machines and the various websites that she had been scanning, the ones that connected the anaplasmosis, the babesiosis, the ehrlichiosis, and the Lyme disease in ticks to the militarized mycoplasma fermentans incognitus, as well as the ones that showed chilling images of the torture to which the nation in which she

currently lived was subjecting citizens of other nations, were all coursing through her blood, her nerve
meridians, and her intestines, until she was quivering
with some sweet sick feeling. And then a few hours
later, she realized that a small nipple was growing out
of her side, or perhaps just a nipple-like bruise where
the tick had entered her. It was purple and brown and
yellow-white. A red rash surrounded it. It was neither
sore nor itchy. It was simply there, there where it had
not been before, even though it had been only a few
hours, not the two weeks that the Internet had promised it would take before the rash might appear. She
emailed her friend, a friend with experience in alternative remedies and treatments and side effects, and
received the name and contact information of a specialist. The specialist had a website full of information
about the evils of the healthcare industry and various
governmental agencies presented in an aesthetically
pleasing design format that she found reassuring. She
called the specialist's office, made an appointment for
the next afternoon, and returned to her work.

She wasn't sure what she wanted this new composition to sound like, what she wanted it to do. But
she knew what she didn't want. She didn't want it to
be easy to dance to or to be something to march to
or to simply be parsed out in recognizable phrygian

or lydian or dorian or locrian or aeolian modes. She didn't want it to reference endangered birds or privatized drops of water or other things that just made you feel sad. She didn't want it to be spare and lyrical or melodic and rich. She wanted it to be not easy to listen to but also not so hard to listen to that you'd just want to shut it off or want to just read the liner notes and nod your head to the explanations therein, nodding as if to a beat, thinking the right proper political thoughts in the head but not the messy ugly things that stir in the belly or resonate in the inner cavities of a right proper North American body faced with the implications.

So she sat and listened, surfing and watching and clicking and thinking and collecting and downloading and storing, all the while worrying that the tick bite might be throbbing a little too much. She watched testimonies at various government hearings, listening to the cadence and lilt of each voice as much as to the details and the evasive language, the tortured syntax required to reduce what had been done by all of us to the fault of a few. She played several videos simultaneously and from within the din of the white noise and static she isolated and sampled the voice of a lone female protestor interrupting the proceedings by screaming burn it! burn it! burn it! from the back of one of the hearing rooms, before being escorted out by three men, her head forward and down, her spine straight and aligned, her right arm pulled back, her left arm protecting the baby that she was carrying in a sling that hung from her neck. All the while she wondered how a digital sample cut and pasted into a sound piece might somehow capture all that she was now seeing, thinking, feeling, all its implications for her art, her desire for some right action in the world outside her computer, her recording and mixing machines, her office, her own isolated life.

She knew that it would be easy enough to find an audio sample of a jail-cell door being slammed shut, but she wanted the sound of the actual jail-cell door there in the photos on her screen. She found several samples of prison guards shouting, of keys in metal locks, of military-issue mops being sloshed around inside half-filled buckets, but she wanted to hear the actual guards in the actual photos, their voices, their keys, their broom handles. She knew that, regardless of the source, the sounds would be indistinguishable to the computer, just bits of data to be processed, and she knew the sounds would likewise be indistinguishable to the ear, just free-floating, invisible sound waves to be deciphered, but it still mattered to her somehow.

All day long as she worked she felt the tick bite nipple-bruise pulsing with heat in her side. She would pull her cold, cold hands off the keyboard and rub them together to increase her circulation and then run the fingers of one of her hands over the nipple-bruise on her side as she squirmed in her seat, trying to focus. Something was changing inside her, something she could not name, as if the tick bite were taking on a life of its own, a pulsing, but whether it was pulsing just the usual things that are in the vomit of a tick, the anaplasmosis, the babesiosis, the eh-rlichiosis, and the Lyme disease, or whether it was also pulsing the militarized mycoplasma fermentans incognitus and the alliances between Nazi and U.S. military germ warfare technologies, or whatever biological contagions might mutate as a result of the shame and anger and rage she felt as a citizen artist, she could not say.

The next morning she woke up feverish and weak, but she still drove to the specialist's office. The specialist's name was Laura. She was healthy and fit, her eyes creased reassuringly when she smiled, and she had an easy manner. She had an interest in healing and in using a light touch and alternative methods to stimulate the body to cleanse all that the environment deposits or stirs up within.

She showed Laura the nipple-like bruise with its bull's-eye pattern and Laura fingered it gently. Laura then had her clench one hand into a fist and hold it out in the air while she did some applied kinesiology, pressing down on her arm to test her resistance, all the while whispering questions, seemingly more to the tick bite than to her. "You smell," Laura eventually said. "Thin layers of sweat across the skin. Sweet and metallic." She then had her lie down while she held a series of slides above her head, projecting each through a magnifying lens in order to read the immune system. Each slide was a photograph of a different kind of tick-borne disease, Laura explained, as she put down the lens and then held a tiny speaker over her belly and broadcast the amplified sound of the various parasites of the kind the tick had released in her, which sounded like the sounds trapped within the dead spaces of her composition, sounds she'd been unable to isolate or remove from the master mix.

"You have something living inside you," Laura said. "And there's no cure. I cannot fix you," she said, "it cannot be cut out of you. And you will be sharing it with others for the rest of your life."

Laura smiled softly, reassuringly, and handed her an ice pack for her tick-bite nipple. "Don't worry," she said, "what's in you is not you. But the militarized

mycoplasma fermentans incognitus is in your spiro-
chetes and it will always adapt and mutate, will always be one step ahead of you."

The next day, per the specialist's instructions for
lowering her fever, she drove to the local ice rink,
parked her car and went inside, paid the attendant,
a man whose nametag identified him as Mel, then
walked out onto the ice with her yoga mat and lay
down on the cold, cold ice. She lay on her back and
felt the cold ice beneath her and did thirty sit-ups.
She took several deep breaths, trying to breathe into
the felt-sense of the tick-bite nipple growing on her
side, throbbing with heat, and then she tried to relax
her neck into the cold ice and breathe into a felt-
sense of her hometown, cold and lonesome in the
winter, while doing another thirty sit-ups. Then she
breathed into the felt-sense of how the militarized
mycoplasma fermentans incognitus interacted with
the anaplasmosis, the babesiosis, the ehrlichiosis,
and the Lyme disease inside her and, as she did this,
she pressed her feet firmly into the yoga mat and
did another thirty sit-ups. Then she breathed into
a felt-sense of screaming burn it, burn it, burn it,
while doing yet another thirty sit-ups on the cold,
cold ice. She repeated this remedy until her thinking
and her breathing seemed to fuse into a bodily-felt

sensation, a cool, blue mist that also was warming, fluid, expansive.

That afternoon, she was back at her office, grading papers, filling out forms, going to meetings, answering emails, turning in expense accounts and travel reimbursement forms, notating student compositions, reading a colleague's report on admissions and matriculation trends, signing off on a new department initiative, reading and commenting on student dissertation chapters, writing various recommendation letters, reading announcements of upcoming concerts and performances, stopping occasionally to record some sound coming from her machines or to toggle the joystick and adjust the levels, all the while pressing the icepack against her tick-bite nipple and breathing into a felt-sense of hot anger, shame, and frustration.

As she continued to struggle with her piece, she became increasingly hot and a little weak. The fever was high enough to make her feel slightly confused as she went about her day. It made her feel things she had not felt before. She didn't like finding herself tapping her foot as she graded papers or nodding her head as she signed forms in triplicate, but it seemed impossible for her to do otherwise. The fever did not incapacitate her. It seemed to energize her. She wanted to write beyond her aloneness, to make music of and for a shared anger, of and for some larger we, for how we feel violence coming at us from every side and threatening to infect us. But she did not know how to get the composition to itch in the hot blood of the ear-meat and rut in the lower chakras, to make in her or anyone a pulse to action, one that could be assembled into song if song were to be stinging, one that might skip a beat and jolt the heart in heat and fury and then stutter-strut in some unquiet riot, so that she might allow herself to nod her head after all, head banging in fuck-all dread-lust, fist raised and slam dancing till all the prisons burned down. None of this seemed possible, but that was what she wanted as a possibility.

In that imaginary and symbolic raised fist, she envisioned a hand clenching a brown-black baton, and then she wanted that too, wanted the sound of a baton being brought down in rage and smashing through her samplers and her drum machines, or the sound of a prison guard's baton slamming against the metal bars of a cell, or the sound of the baton being brought down on a body, the sound of the dense plastic of the straight-stick meeting the flesh and bone, a sound somewhere between cracking and thudding. As she fingered her tick bite nipple-bruise with her left hand, she clicked with her right to an online video showing a group of soldiers beating a hooded man with their sticks. As she watched the video she zoomed in, focusing on the welts and wounds on the shirtless body, target-shaped bruises and raised bumps dissolving into dark washes of pixels the closer she zoomed. She began to nod her head to the disjointed up-and-down motion of each prison guard's arm, zooming in and out until the batons became drumsticks and her head banged against the desk, making a sound somewhere in between thudding and cracking. She turned the sound down on the video and then pressed the record button on the sampler and began to pound her head against the mic in time to the blows in the video, as the stacks of papers and files jostled and fell to the floor. With each crack and each thud she felt herself wanting more, harder and louder, until it began to feel like it was she who was in control of the rising and falling batons on the screen.

Next she added sections of "Cum on Feel the Noize" and "Girls, Girls, Girls," arena rock anthems that the military police would pump full volume into the cell blocks late at night to keep the detainees sleep-deprived, the same songs that she had listened to over and over years ago while working graveyard shift at a bail bonds office across the street from the county jailhouse in her hometown. She remembered how in order to stay awake all night she'd played the songs so many times that she would have to open her bright yellow Walkman and untwist the magnetic tape inside the cassette, wondering at how such music could be reduced to such crinkly material, a wonderment that somehow connected to her being here today, in her office chair, a composer with responsibilities and a day job and student loan debt and even, at moments, a desire to know what it would be like to fuck someone in the back seat of an American-made car before he or she left for overseas military service, heavy metal pulsing from the speakers and the sound of metal keys jangling from the ignition as the car rocked back and forth.

Then she thought she might compose the piece with the sounds around her instead, the sounds that, if she listened closely enough, were also the sounds of what she was seeing on the screen, that were related somehow, even if they sounded very different to the computer or the ear. The actual sounds of her being here now in her office, in her life, her side pulsing hot where the tick bite had swollen into a bruised nipple, the sounds of the connectivity with and distance from what she saw and heard on the screen. So not just the sound of machine-gun fire, percussive and violent, but the sounds of cars and trucks that passed by her all day and night, the gas-fueled cars and trucks that she thought of as connected to the sound of machine-gun fire, just as she sometimes thought of her hand as some kind of flesh-gun using her joystick to direct a remote-controlled drone over the oil refineries in Basra. And not just the sound of bombs dropping from the sky onto roads or bridges or checkpoints or airfields or weapons facilities or villages or wedding celebrations, screeching and whistling and then deep and booming, but also the sound of the whirring fan inside her computer that kept the hard drive and the circuit boards from overheating, the computer that gave her access to these sounds that she would listen to but not use, sounds that were and were not hers, sounds that were inside her ears and brain and body cavities whether she sampled them or not.

And so she continued working like this for many more days and through it all the tick bite continued to throb. Each day she would grab the sampler's joy-stick and point and click and drag and drop, all the while gazing at the screen, its pulsing pixels chart-ing levels and durations in the mix, thinking about how the things that were in there, the pain and the labor and the keys in the locks and the mops in the buckets, could become so abstracted, how a body's sounds could be reduced to data matrices and information flows and unmoored sounds and colors and vague signals and sensations on her screen and in her brain, in her bloodstream and her guts, in her well-fed, white, and fleshy body.

Eventually, she went back to see the specialist. She said to Laura, "Why do you think I'm so miserable? My compositions are full of responsibilities, bad history, the stink of shit and gasoline on my hands. I'm burning up but not burning it down. I can't think, I can't compose, I can't write. Not only am I not in control of my thoughts, they're not even my thoughts."

Laura smiled patiently as she ran her through the remedies, reminding her to breathe deeply into her body and find the felt-sense of impasse and contagion, of cool light and inner sonority.

"Like cures like," she said, as she squeezed a dropperful of some strange liquid beneath her tongue. "You have to get out of your head, explore how your body finds its remedy. Let your tick bite quiver and cast its spells," she said. "Finger your knobs and buttons lightly, and then squeeze until all expresses all."

The next day she drove again to the downtown ice rink, went inside, paid Mel, and then walked with her yoga mat to lie down on the cold, cold ice. She lay on her back and felt the ice beneath her and began her remedy of thirty sit-ups. She took several deep breaths, breathing into her felt-sense of pregnant prison guards with batons in their fists and weaponized tick-infected breastmilk and then tried to relax her neck into the cold ice and breathe into her felt-sense of warm bass tones vibrating her subwoofers, flowing through her and melting the ice. She would press her tail into the cold ice and think of the numbers that made her feel tense, statistics and symptoms and secret military deals that would turn up in both her composition and her vaginal discharge, or the amplified sounds coming from the bacteria in the insects in the machines in her office, or if she'd had her period since the tick bite. She repeated this remedy until her trying and her breathing and her thinking began once more to converge into a bodily-felt sensation, a crisp pink flare that was also cool, aerated, propulsive, the shaking and vibrations in her throat and spine producing some strange voice not her own that whispered, "rage and spit, rage and spit." The ice rink had the felt-sense of anger and shame but also of release and achievement. The ice rink was something inside her that was and was not her. And the ice rink felt good. But the ice rink was also stasis and acceptance, not action. The ice rink was no remedy.

The next day, she was back in her office chair, her head throbbing in the sick light of the computer screen, which was bookmarked to a webpage on remedy testing. Her desk was strewn with various forms, sheet music, essays, letters of recommendation, draft liner notes, interdepartmental memos, healthcare reimbursement forms, photocopied articles concerning illicit and covert military operations conducted in North Africa, and a color photograph she had downloaded from the Internet.

The woman in the photo was from her hometown. The woman in the photo had gotten out just like she had, but instead of leaving for college as she had, the woman in the photo had left for the army, for the job. She tried to make eye contact with the woman through the surface of the photograph, tried to mirror the half-smile, half-smirk with her own mouth. Rubbing the spot on her body where the tick had left its target, she closed her eyes and imagined the woman back home instead, in a high school yearbook photo, thumbs up at a pep rally or outside the metal shop with the long-haired boys, faint wisps of teenage mustaches on their upper lips, a Mötley Crüe T-shirt hanging limply off the skinnier one's frame, wires leading from his ears to a bright yellow Walkman gripped in his hand, or hanging at the lake in cutoffs, an unlit cigarette dangling from the corner of her half-smiling, half-smirking mouth.

She wanted the sound of that high school yearbook photo in her piece. She wanted the sound of whatever it sounded like to leave one's hometown and go wherever one goes to end up across the globe and in different photos with a gun and a cigarette and a job to do. The sound of becoming a Specialist First Class. The sound of following orders. The sound of the click of the camera and the sound of the smell of the yearbook pages when you crack it open one last time in the concrete parking lot outside the school before leaving for good.

She wanted the sound of this woman's pregnancy, too, invisible there in the photo yet there all the same. She wanted the sound of the zipper on the body bag in the photo, the sound of the zipper as she pulled it down, releasing the heat and the scent of the bruised body within, and the sound of the corpse as it jostled the ice cubes put inside the bag to keep it cold. She wanted to put the words of the woman's later testimony in her own mouth, to speak them into a bottle of ice-cold water and then keep the now frozen words in a freezer powered by electricity garnered from the burning of coal mined from the mountains where she and the woman both grew up, mountains and mines memorialized in a book by Muriel Rukeyser that she used to read in bed with an old lover, years ago, in the cold, cold winter, in a small apartment kept warm by an old leaky oil heater.

But above all, she wanted the sound of that thumbs-up. She wanted to hear it in the mix. She wanted the song to quiver with the blood pulse that courses from one's heart up the chest and then through the shoulder and down the arm, through the wrist and meat of the hand and then up the thumb to beat at its very tip. She wanted that upturned thumb in her composition, wanted to insert it into the whole, wanted it to be there wiggling and thrusting and pushing and waving and sticking in the brain-meat and then to hold the thumb there as if poised to press down on a lighter-flint, ready to flare up and salute the whole goddamn show, the pep rally, the arena rock anthem, the flag ceremony, and then to set it all aflame, to burn it all down, leaving only the sound of photographs melting into glitter and ash.

She sat back from the screen and, with her right hand, she turned on the microphone and hit record, then guided the mouse to open up her Facebook account, proceeding to click-like everything she could find, watching as the thumbs-up would appear after each mechanical click. She click-liked the Military

Displays & Patriotic Music by the Bel Air Community Chorus Facebook page and she click-liked the StopIslamofascism Facebook page. She click-liked the NEA Jazz Masters page and she click-liked the National Flag Month page. She click-liked the Tipper Sticker page and she click-liked the US Army Mothers page. She click-liked the GetLoFi page and she click-liked the Improvised Explosive Device page. She click-liked National Youth Orchestra of Iraq and she click-liked the Bagram Air Base page. She click-liked the Kid Rock page and she click-liked the American Military Academy page.

She clicked and waited for the thumbs-up icon, clicked and watched, then onto the next page, the next click, the next thumbs-up. She moved the mouse with her right hand until the arrow hit its target and then she squeezed and pressed and heard the click, and she liked this. All the clicks sounded the same but they also sounded different somehow. Either way, she liked them all.

She saved the recording and dumped the file into the master, lining up the click-track with the other samples to provide a kind of nervous subchatter, like the sound of masticating insects burrowing their pincers into her flesh, or the sound of the Internet itself, tiny circuits toggling on and off, endless variations of signals feeding her the millions of pixels necessary to bring the ice-cold images to her screen. She slowly released the mouse, her sweaty hand cramped and twisted inward like a claw, the thumb jutting out like the tick-bite nipple on her side. She downloaded the sound file onto her thumb drive and then threw it into her bag, along with a stack of student papers, the employee healthcare rules and restrictions guidebook, three departmental course proposals, a collection of essays on appropriation, and then, her palms sweaty and her mouth thirsty and hot and her teeth grinding out sublingual rhythms, she headed home.

That night, she tried to sit down and write a description of her composition. She wanted to be able to stop writing in her liner notes pithy statements about the relationship between her music and endangered species or natural resources or imperialism. She wanted to write about it in a way to somehow make the right political action flare up inside, coming out of the music to fuel the supercharged struggle-force that would give forth the impulse and strength to flip over a dozen police cars and then start a crazy dance party in the emptied parking spaces. She wanted to explain all this, to explain how all this could be inside something that might otherwise just sound like jumbled noise. But it kept coming out wrong.

She remembered Laura saying, don't listen to your mind, listen to your meat. So, lying in her bed and sweating from fever, she plugged the thumb drive into her laptop and then connected the laptop to her stereo and hit play, and as she closed her eyes and listened she tried to visualize the still reverberating clicks and pixelated thumbs moving down the inside of her body. She breathed deeply, into the felt-sense of all that was brewing inside her, the bacterial frenzy, the humming and the feed, a pulsing for art and an impulse to action. What she thought had been stray samples buried in the mix, pulp prosodies choking on the standard operating procedures, she now realized were guttural sounds bubbling up from deep inside her, coalescing into deep fevered whispers that seemed to be both inside and outside her, spitting out stuttered spasms of slammed jail-cell doors, shouting prison guards, keys in locks, military-issue mops sloshing in the slop buckets.

Then she heard, emanating from her throat chakra, a voice saying, "I contain a strange liquid in me. I see bodies rolling in shit, thin layers of sweat across the skin in whatever genders we are, the muscles around my esophagus beginning to move. Still, I'm scared to follow my desires in this sick society, even though it only takes four or five to make a band, instrumental or not. If I'm constantly terrorized by the images on the screen and starved by the law, I cannot rock and I cannot cum." And then, from her sacral chakra, a deep resonant chamber seemed to fill with gas and, in a slow release that ran through the entirety of her digestive tract, the voice continued, saying, "We are anti-dharma in heat, caking your intestines with slow-cooking resin, waiting to be scraped, harvested, and smoked in the pipe your friend brought back from Kabul, or else we ask you to send in the living cultures and use the enema runoff to feed your food, the moist and pulpy garden soil pulling toxins from the roots of all that might yet simmer and stew in the soup." And then the voice moved down to her root chakra, where she heard the electronic buzz of her computer and the fluorescent office lights cross fading into her interior body-static to make a white noise that crystallized into a feverish fine mist, one that crackled like the sound of interrogation videos being systematically destroyed, the magnetic tape twisted and yanked from its plastic casing by pairs of pale nail-bitten hands. Resonating inside her she could now hear the tracks popping and repeating out of sync, as if multiple record players were skipping inside an emptied-out military gymnasium, and she could hear amidst

the anxious gurgling a faint moaning, a female voice
whimpering and gasping, "zip up and shut up, sit up
and spit up, zip up and shut up, sit up and spit up,"
whether in distress or pleasure she could not tell, but
there nonetheless.

The next morning she called in sick to work and
drove directly to the specialist's office. Laura smiled
a sad yet patient smile and asked her to lie down on
the table while she held a Lucite block over her third-
eye chakra, placing various small glass bottles on it,
each containing a diluted remedy, while whispering a
poem through the block, seemingly more to the remedies than to her:

Make me well, I said,—And the delighted
    touch.
You put dead sweet hand on my dead brain.
The window cleared and the night-street stood
    black.
As soon as I left your house others besieged me
forcing my motion, saying, Make me well.

Took sickness into the immense street,
but nothing was thriving I saw blank light the
    crazy
blink of torture the lack and there is no

personal sickness strong to intrude there.
Returned. Stood at the window. Make me well.

Putting away her Lucite block and her remedies, Laura said, "As I said before, I cannot cure you. No one can cure you. You can't cure you. I can modulate your fever, but what is there inside you will still come; it's growing inside you, it's the you that's not you that's coming. And you can let it suck the life out of you or you can find in it fuel for action. Make the song-sound of your body and its yearning," she said, "for art and for health, and lead us in feverish symphonies consisting of the application and abrupt removal of duct tape from the mouth and the agitation of the bruises caused by renegade acupuncture treatments, and then rub it all vigorously with a back-and-forth motion and go out moving through the world with a tenfold increase in interest in it, because everything that happens to you and by you, here in your body and out there in the world, all that everything is in you now, and all that everything should be in your song."

Laura paused, took a deep breath and exhaled. "I will explain this to you with a story," she said. "Try to understand this. This is not an allegory. You go every day to the ice rink for your sit-ups, but after you leave there is a free skate period that's open to the public.

You might barely notice Mel, the man who takes your ticket, but during the free skate Mel must smooth the ice every couple of hours. He will open two swinging side panels on the south end of the ice rink, mount a Zamboni and guide it out to do his rounds. The skaters are forced to exit the rink as he does this, and they go to visit the concession stand or restrooms or just stand and watch him. He drives in a clockwise motion of slightly overlapping ovals, taking care to guide the motion of the machine like a skater rather than drive it like a car. It takes him between six and seven minutes to do the eight full passes around the ice. While he glides along, the DJ always blasts "Ice, Ice, Baby" and sometimes the younger skaters who are watching cheer and wave at him as he slowly passes by them on his lumbering machine.

"His shift has its own rhythms, like anything else. After the ice is resurfaced, he returns to his perch at the door, selling tickets and directing visitors to the skate rental desk or the restrooms. He works in isolation, usually reading, no one to talk with, no union meetings or drinks with the co-workers after work. He is paid minimum wage and has no health insurance, no pension. He mostly lives paycheck to paycheck. When the kids enter or leave the rink, passing him at his desk, they often call him Zamboni

Man and sometimes they might sing a line or two from the song, his song. He nods halfheartedly and returns to his book, thinking ahead to when his wife will pick him up on her way home from work, the last of the day's sunlight filtering through the kitchen windows as they sit at the table in the shared weary silence of love after work.

"But right now, as I am talking to you, the machine is sputtering and smoking, the engine kicking and choking. He has to stop, dismount, walk around on the ice in his street shoes, and open the hood. He reaches in and his hands are immediately coated with oozing hot, black oil. The rear main bearing has been pounded out from excessive endplay. The main bearing, the one closest to the flywheel, has worn out, worn out in two directions, one parallel to the crankshaft and the other perpendicular. The perpendicular force has worn the main-bearing bore so that the crankshaft has begun to wobble, which in turn has distorted the neoprene oil seal at the bearing bore, and the oil is now pouring through it and onto his worn leather work gloves. He pulls his hands out and stands there, breathing heavily, looking at his gloves as the oil pools and drips down onto the cold, cold ice."

WHAT WE TALK ABOUT
WHEN WE TALK ABOUT POETRY

MY FRIEND MEL MCGINNIS was talking. Mel McGinnis is a poet, and sometimes that gives him the right.

The four of us were sitting around his kitchen table drinking gin. Sunlight filled the kitchen from the big window behind the sink. There were Mel and me and his second wife, Teresa—Terri, we called her—and my wife, Laura. We were all writers and we lived in the Bay Area, then. But we were all from somewhere else.

There was an ice bucket on the table. The gin and the tonic water kept going around, and we somehow got on the subject of poetry. Mel thought real poetry had nothing to do with politics. He said he'd spent years union organizing before quitting to go to graduate school. He said he still looked back on those years in the union as the most important in his life.

Terri said the man she lived with before she lived with Mel was a poet. Then Terri said, "He was really political and he talked about poetry all the time. He would not stop talking about *A*, you know, Zukofsky's poem. He kept saying it was the greatest poem ever written. He would quote it when we were in bed. 'An impulse to action sings of resemblances,' or whatever it was." Terri looked around the table. "What do you do with a man like that?"

She was a bone-thin woman with a pretty face, dark eyes, and brown hair that hung down her back. She liked poetry, but she liked the poets more. She liked the parties.

"My God, don't be silly. That stuff he was quoting made you hot and that was it, and you know it," Mel said. "I don't know what you'd call it, but I sure know you wouldn't call it political. It was poetry, that's all."

"Say what you want to, but there was a politics," Terri said. "It may sound crazy to you, but it's true just the same. People are different, Mel. Sure, sometimes this poet may have written crazy. Okay. But he wrote political poetry. In his own way, maybe, but he wrote it. There was politics there, Mel. Don't say there wasn't."

Mel let out his breath. He held his glass and turned to Laura and me. "The man kept quoting Marx . . . Marx," Mel said. He finished his drink and reached for the gin bottle. "Terri's a romantic. Terri's of the 'Give-me-a-bunch-of-lines-about-capitalism-so-I'll-know-it's-serious' school. Terri, hon, don't look that way." Mel reached across the table and touched Terri's cheek with his fingers. He grinned at her.

"Now he wants to make up," Terri said.

"Make up what?" Mel said. "What is there to make up? I know what I know. That's all."

"How'd we get started on this subject anyway?" Terri said. She raised her glass and drank from it. "Mel always has poetry on his mind," she said. "Don't you, honey?" She smiled, and I thought that was the last of it.

"I just wouldn't call Zukofsky's uptight aesthetics political. That's all I'm saying, honey," Mel said. "What about you guys?" Mel said to Laura and me. "Does it seem political to you?"

"I'm the wrong person to ask," I said. "I write fiction. I don't even know the man, or his poetry. I've only heard his name. I wouldn't know. You'd have to know all the particulars."

Mel said, "The kind of poetry I'm talking about moves you. The kind of poetry I'm talking about, you don't try to talk about Marxism."

Laura said, "I don't know anything about Zukofsky. I thought only boys read him."

I touched the back of Laura's hand. She gave me a quick smile. I picked up Laura's hand. It was warm, the nails short, unpolished, practical. I encircled the broad wrist with my fingers, and I held her.

"His work did have politics," Terri said. She clasped her arms with her hands. "And it is meaningful to many people. They talk about it. They use it to talk with each other. That's a kind of politics. My God," Terri said. She waited a minute, then let go of her arms and picked up her glass.

"What people won't say to get a little action!" Laura said.

"He's out of the action now," Mel said. "Laura's right. No one reads him but a bunch of white guys in Buffalo or whatever."

Mel handed me the saucer of limes. I took a section, squeezed it over my drink, and stirred the ice cubes with my finger.

"But his work's still meaningful," Terri said. "It isn't like his work stopped capitalism. But it still means something to people. It still moves them," she said. Terri shook her head.

"Poor Zukofsky nothing," Mel said. "He wasn't political."

Mel was forty-five years old. He was tall and rangy with curly soft hair. He looked like the poet-

professor that he was. When he was sober, his ges-
tures, all his movements, were precise, very careful.

"He knew how to write, Mel. Grant me that,"
Terri said. "That's all I'm asking. He didn't write the
way you write. I'm not saying that. But he knew how
to write. You can grant me that, can't you?"

"What do you mean, 'He knew how to write'?"
I said.

Laura leaned forward with her glass. She put
her elbows on the table and held her glass in both
hands. She glanced from Mel to Terri and waited
with a look of bewilderment on her open face, as
if amazed that such things happened to people you
were friendly with.

"What do you mean he knew how to write?" I
said.

"I'll tell you what he did," Mel said. "In one part
of the book, 'A-9,' he took this form from this classi-
cal poet Cavalcanti, this canzone. He took it because
this Jew-hating poet that he looked up to was ob-
sessed with it. I'm serious. He was the child of Jew-
ish immigrants. He grew up speaking Yiddish. And
then he writes a poem in English using an old Italian
form that this fascist poet that he looked up to had
translated. Can you believe it? A guy like him? But he
did. See, he was devoted to the tradition, to the form.

And so he writes a double canzone, with complicated rhymes and meters. But he makes his poem about labor and love. And he uses the words of Marx to write his poem, he takes Marx and some other writers and he collages the words all together in this complex way to fit the form. But the poem makes no regular sense. The language is all weird and stilted. He puns on the words 'pit,' 'capitalism,' and 'capitulation.' Little things like that. It uses political words, but that doesn't make it political."

"I still feel it when I read it," Terri said.

"But what does it mean?" Laura said. "What do you mean you can feel it?"

Laura is a writer, or might someday be a writer. We'd met in a professional capacity. In the classroom. Before we knew it, it was a courtship. She's twenty-five, fifteen years younger than I am. In addition to being in love, we like each other and enjoy one another's company. She's easy to be with.

"What does it mean?" Laura asked again.

Mel said, "He wanted to say something about labor, and about love. The poem is about how, if things could speak, they'd have the voices of the people who made them, not just those who own them, you know, like this table here, Marx, all that. But that's the first canzone. Ten years later, after he's married and has a kid, he writes the second part and it's about love."

"So the love rewrites the labor part?" Laura said.

"Some say that," Terri said. "But I think they're together in the poem. That love is labor."

"He was abstract," Mel said. "The music's there, but the meaning, it's all jumbled. If you call that political, you can have it."

"Oh, it's political," Terri said. "Sure it's abstract in most people's eyes. But he felt he needed to write it like that."

"I sure as hell wouldn't call it political," Mel said. "I mean, it's clever, it's poetic, but no one knows what he did it for. I've seen a lot of poems, and I couldn't say anyone ever knew what they did it for."

Mel put his hands behind his neck and tilted his chair back. "I'm not interested in that kind of politics," he said. "If that's political, you can keep it."

Terri said, "In the poem, love is part of the resistance to capitalism. It's about labor as well as love. Labor gets defined by love, a love that is care and attention to the processes of work."

Terri drank from her glass. She said, "But Mel's right—the poem is abstract. It's very formal, but also political. It is all about politics and yet its language is hard to follow. The form pushes away meaning. That pushing away is part of the meaning, maybe. But also in the second half, where the love comes in stronger, after he gets married, it's where he gets all domestic, like us here, out of the union hall and here at the kitchen table. Isn't that a laugh?" Terri said.

She poured the last of the gin into her glass and waggled the bottle. Mel got up from the table and went to the cupboard. He took down another bottle.

"Well, Nick and I know what good writing is," Laura said. "For us, I mean," Laura said. She bumped my knee with her knee. "You're supposed to say something now," Laura said, and turned her smile on me.

For an answer, I took Laura's hand and raised it to my lips. I made a big production out of kissing her hand. Everyone was amused.

"We're lucky," I said.

"You guys," Terri said. "Stop that now. You're making me sick. You're still on a honeymoon, for God's sake. You're still gaga, for crying out loud. Just wait. How long have you been together now? How long has it been? A year? Longer than a year."

"Going on a year and a half," Laura said, flushed and smiling.

"Oh, now," Terri said. "Wait a while."

She held her drink and gazed at Laura.

"I'm only kidding," Terri said.

Mel opened the gin and went around the table with the bottle.

"Here, you guys," he said. "Let's have a toast. I want to propose a toast. A toast to poetry. To true poetry," Mel said.

We touched glasses.

"To poetry, true poetry," we said.

Outside, in the backyard, one of the dogs began to bark. The leaves of the aspen that leaned past the window ticked against the glass. The afternoon sunlight was like a presence in this room, the spacious light of ease and generosity. We could have been anywhere, somewhere enchanted. We raised our glasses again and grinned at each other like children who had agreed on something forbidden.

"I'll tell you about politics and poetry," Mel said. "I mean, I'll give you a good example. And then you can draw your own conclusions." He poured more gin into his glass. He added an ice cube and a sliver of lime. We waited and sipped our drinks. Laura and I touched knees again. I put a hand on her warm thigh and left it there.

"What do any of us really know about poetry?" Mel said. "It seems to me we're just beginners at poetry. We say we write and we do, I don't doubt it. I've read Nick and Nick's read me. But what do we know about the kind of poetry I'm talking about now. The stuff we all read and call avant-garde. Sometimes I have a hard time accounting for the fact that I loved the more traditional stuff too. But I did, I know I did." He thought about it and then he went on. "There was a time when I thought I loved that Mary Oliver poem about the geese more than life itself. The one with the line about how 'You only have to let the soft animal of your body love what it loves.' But now I find it corny. I do. How do you explain that? What happened to that love? What happened to it, is what I'd like to know. I wish someone could tell me. Then there's Zukofsky. Okay, we're back to him. He loves his wife and his son so much that he winds up writing a canzone about that love and then Terri's boyfriend quotes it to her in bed." Mel stopped talking and swallowed from his glass. "That's the issue. Who would you read in bed to each other? Yes, that's the real issue. I used to know this woman and we would read Ernesto Cardenal in bed at night. For an entire year we read a few pages each night from Cardenal. Not because he did fancy things with Marx, or counted his syllables just so, but because that guy believed in the world. Am I wrong? Am I way off base? Because I want you to set me straight if you think I'm wrong. I want to know. I mean, I don't know anything, and I'm the first one to admit it."

"Mel, for God's sake," Terri said. She reached out and took hold of his wrist. "Are you getting drunk? Honey? Are you drunk?"

"Honey, I'm just talking," Mel said. "All right? I don't have to be drunk to say what I think. I mean, we're all just talking, right?" Mel said. He fixed his eyes on her.

"Sweetie, I'm not criticizing," Terri said.

She picked up her glass.

"I'm not driving home," Mel said. "Let me remind you of that. I am not driving."

"Mel, we love you," Laura said.

Mel looked at Laura. He looked at her as if he couldn't place her, as if she was not the woman she was.

"Love you too, Laura," Mel said. "And you, Nick, love you too. You know something?" Mel said. "You guys are our pals," Mel said.

He picked up his glass.

Mel said, "I was going to tell you about something. I mean, I was going to prove a point about poetry. You see, that poem was written a number of years ago, but things like it are still being written right now, and it ought to make us feel ashamed when we talk like we know what we're talking about when we talk about poetry and politics."

"Come on now," Terri said. "Don't talk like you're drunk if you're not drunk."

"Just shut up for once in your life," Mel said very quietly. "Will you do me a favor and do that for a minute? So as I was saying, in Bhopal, in like 1984 or so, maybe 15,000 people died? Union Carbide, right? Gas leak all over the place."

Terri looked at us and then back at Mel. She seemed anxious, or maybe that's too strong a word.

Mel was handing the bottle around the table.

"I remember when it happened," Mel said. "The workers are cleaning the pipes and then there's a re-action, an explosion, a leak, whatever. About thirty minutes later, people start suffocating, coughing. Their eyes burning. They're vomiting. People trampled trying to escape. By morning, thousands are dead. There were mass funerals and mass cremations. Buffalo, goats, dead animals all over the place. Leaves on the trees falling off and all that."

"Folks, this is an advertisement for the National Not Poetry Society," Terri said. "This is your spokes-man, Doctor Melvin R. McGinnis, talking about the meaninglessness of poetry." Terri laughed. "Mel," she said, "sometimes you're just too much. But I love you, honey," she said.

"Honey, I love you," Mel said.

He leaned across the table. Terri met him half-way. They kissed.

"Terri's right," Mel said as he settled himself again. "I don't need to retell the story. But seriously, this story is about why I think poetry doesn't make anything happen."

He drank from his glass. "I'll try to keep this short," he said. "Years before all this, in West Virginia, the same Union Carbide dug a three-mile tunnel under a mountain. So the workers hit a, what's it, a silica deposit. They're not given any masks, even though everyone knew that the miners needed masks. But Union Carbide doesn't bother. So, surprise, most of the workers are all dead within a year. Okay, so, Muriel Rukeyser, now here's your political poet, Muriel Rukeyser writes a poem about it. The poem is fucking beautiful, full of clear language, no need to quote Marx to get the point across. It opens with the poet going down into the valley. She takes the words of the wives of the dead miners and she turns it into this lyric song. There's your 'sings an impulse to action' or whatever. It is impossible not to be moved by this poem. It is a clear, strong poem. A famous poem. People read it. And it did nothing. Fifty years later, Union Carbide, Bhopal, boom, nothing."

Mel stopped talking. "Here," he said, "let's drink

this cheapo gin the hell up. Then we're going to dinner right? Terri and I know a new place. That's where we'll go, to this new place we know about. But we're not going until we finish up this cut-rate, lousy gin."

Terri said, "We haven't actually gone there yet. But it looks good. From the outside, you know."

"I like pretty words, end of day," Mel said. "If I had it to do all over again, I'd be a lyric poet, you know? Right, Terri?" Mel said. "Tell me about your despair, yours, and I'll tell you mine. But make it pretty." He laughed. He fingered the ice in his glass.

"Terri knows. Terri can tell you. But let me say this. If I could come back again in a different life, a different time and all, you know what? I'd like to come back as Sappho. Playing the lyre. She was ugly, but still it's alright as long you've got women and song."

"Mel likes to pretend he'd have Sappho's skills with the ladies," Terri said.

"Calling them to him with his poetry," Laura said.

"Or just wants to be a woman," Mel said.

"Shame on you," Laura said.

Terri said, "Suppose you came back as Homer. Blind bards didn't have it so good in those days," Terri said.

"Epic poets never had it good," Mel said. "Writing for the tribe. But I guess even Sappho was a vessel to someone. Isn't that the way it worked? But then everyone is a vessel to someone else. Isn't that right? Terri? But what I like about Sappho, besides her love of women and her ugliness, was that there was no Union Carbide, you know? No unregulated chemical companies."

"Vassals," Terri said.

"What?" Mel said.

"Vassals," Terri said. "They were called vassals, not vessels."

"Vassals, vessels," Mel said, "what the fuck's the difference? You knew what I meant anyway. All right," Mel said. "So I didn't grow up going to the symphony. I learned my stuff on the shop floor. I'm a poet, sure, got my degree, but I know I'm just a mechanic dressed up as a poet. Kids pay their money and then turn in their poems and I go in and I fuck around and I move a comma or a period, give them back to them. Shit," Mel said.

"Modesty doesn't become you," Terri said.

"He's just a humble poet of the people," I said. "But sometimes despite your degrees you can't see how poetry works. I read somewhere that the prisoners at Attica passed around handwritten copies of that Claude McKay sonnet 'If We Must Die,' Mel. They even wrote it on the walls."

"That's terrible," Mel said. "That's a terrible example, Nicky. That's a prison riot in which thirty-nine people died. That poem did nothing for them. Dead."

"Some other vessel," Terri said.

"That's right," Mel said. "Some vassal always comes along and shoots everyone. Or whatever the fuck they want to do."

"Same things we fight over these days," Terri said.

Laura said, "Nothing's changed. Men fighting."

The color was still high in Laura's cheeks. Her eyes were bright. She brought her glass to her lips.

Mel poured himself another drink. He looked at the label closely as if studying a long row of numbers. Then he slowly put the bottle down on the table and reached for the tonic water.

"What about political poetry, Mel?" Laura said. "You didn't finish what you started."

Laura was having a hard time lighting her cigarette. Her matches kept going out.

The sunshine inside the room was different now, changing, getting thinner. But the leaves outside the window were still shimmering, and I stared at the pattern they made on the panes and on the Formica counter. They weren't the same patterns, of course.

"What about politics and poetry?" I said.

"Gets prisoners killed," Terri said.

Mel stared at her.

Terri said, "Go on with your story, hon. I was only kidding. Then what happened?"

"Terri, sometimes," Mel said.

"Please, Mel," Terri said. "Don't always be so serious, sweetie. Can't you take a joke?"

"Where's the joke?" Mel said.

He held his glass and gazed steadily at his wife.

"What about political poetry, seriously?" Laura said.

Mel fastened his eyes on Laura. He said, "Laura, if I didn't have Terri and if I didn't love her so much, and if Nick wasn't my best friend, I'd fall in love with you. I'd write you a sonnet in fourteen iambic and rhyming lines. I'd even keep the politics out, just one hundred percent poetry. Read it to you in bed if you like. I'd carry you off, honey," he said.

"Tell your story," Terri said. "Then we'll go to that new place, okay?"

"Okay," Mel said. "Where was I?" he said. He stared at the table and then he began again. "Here's the thing. There are a lot of things I can say that poetry might as well not do. There is no sense in thinking that if we just find the right form, then the politics will be there. If we just make it lyrical, then it will really move people. Or if we just make it experimental, then it will really shake things up. But the content doesn't seem to matter either. Like it also doesn't mean that if we just make it about the local, it will do something locally. Or if we make it about the workplace, it will help us rise up against capitalism. Or to make it all environmental with long lists of endangered species. Or to write another goddamn Union Carbide poem. I could go on and on listing. It doesn't help to make it a series of clever one-liners about capitalism or the war. Or to make it all about the domestic or love or all explicit about the sex everyone's having. Or make it all about the street or the prison and all edgy and with a funky meter or whatever. I mean the only thing poetry has really done that might matter was in the name of cultural tradition. And tradition only matters when the nation has guns, not just poetry. Because poetry hasn't even been all that convincing to people about the greatness of a nation. Look at all those poets in the Caribbean who make fun of Wordsworth all the time, complaining about having to write poems about daffodils in school, on those islands where daffodils don't even grow."

Mel looked around the table and shook his head at what he was going to say.

"I mean, poetry. It doesn't really do much and that is what makes it so fucking nothing."

We all looked at Mel.

"Do you see what I'm saying?"

Maybe we were a little drunk by then. I know it was hard keeping things in focus. The light was draining out of the room, going back through the window where it had come from. Yet nobody made a move to get up from the table to turn on the overhead light.

"Listen," Mel said. "Let's finish this fucking gin. There's about enough left here for one shooter all around. Then let's go eat. Let's go to the new place."

"He's depressed," Terri said. "Mel, why don't you take a pill?"

Mel shook his head. "I've taken everything there is."

"We all need a pill now and then," I said.

"Some people are born needing them," Terri said. She was using her finger to rub at something on the table. Then she stopped rubbing.

"I think I want to read a poem before we go eat," Mel said. "Is that all right with everybody? I'll read my latest poem," he said.

Terri said, "After that tirade, what would you read? You've just torn down all the things poetry might do. Honey, you know you don't want to read a poem now. It'll make you feel even worse."

"I don't want to talk about poetry," Mel said. "But I want to read a poem, a real poem."

"There isn't a day goes by that Mel doesn't say he wishes he'd stayed organizing rather than teach kids how to write poetry," Terri said. "For one thing," Terri said, "the students only want to talk about themselves. Mel says they just want to write poetry about themselves. If it isn't about them, they don't want to read it. Real poetry doesn't matter to them."

"They don't read real poetry," Mel said. "And if I'm not complaining about having to read their bad poems, then I'm complaining because they haven't turned them in so I can't read them."

"Shame on you," Laura said. "I was one of those students, you know."

"They're bad," Mel said. "Not you, honey, but the rest of 'em. Nick knows, don't you Nicky. Sometimes I think I'll sit down and take my red pen and cross out every line in their precious poems. I'll cross out every line and write a big fat fucking F on the top and then give it back to them."

He crossed one leg over the other. Then he put both feet on the floor and leaned forward, elbows on the table, his chin cupped in his hands.

"Maybe I won't read a poem, after all. Maybe it isn't such a hot idea. Maybe we'll just go eat. How does that sound?"

"Sounds fine to me," I said. "Eat or not eat. Or keep drinking. I could head right on out into the sunset."

"What does that mean, honey?" Laura said.

"It just means what I said," I said. "It means I could just keep going. That's all it means."

"I could eat something myself," Laura said. "I don't think I've ever been so hungry in my life. Is there something to nibble on?"

"I'll put out some cheese and crackers," Terri said.

But Terri just sat there. She did not get up to get anything.

Mel turned his glass over. He spilled it out on the table.

"Gin's gone," Mel said.

Terri said, "Now what?"

I could hear my heart beating. I could hear everyone's heart. I could hear the human noise we sat there making, not one of us moving, not even when the room went dark.

THE SIDE EFFECT

HE FELT WHAT MOST people feel. Lack of affect. An inability to get up and be out in the world. Everything dulled, yet everything full of anxiety. An abject tilt to the head, a slumping of the shoulders, a placing of the right hand over the forehead, and a rubbing of the area of the forehead and eyes with a strong squeezing motion. An inward focus of the brain-place. Anger. Rage. Self-contempt. A desire for cessation, for un-life.

He was otherwise generally agreeable. At least when he was among others, or at least when he was among others and drinking. He had agreed to be agreeable in that way that most of us agree to be agreeable, to keep our diagnoses inside, or to put one diagnosis out into the air among others, in order to mask the more shameful other diagnoses.

Nonetheless, after a fifteen-minute visit with a doctor in a sterile, overly lit office, he agreed that it might be best to inhibit his voltage-sensitive sodium channels, and through this, attempt to stabilize his neuronal membranes and consequently modulate pre-synaptic transmitter releases of excitatory amino acids such as glutamate and aspartate. It seemed reasonable to try this, or at least as reasonable as anything else.

A signed slip of paper made possible this inhibition. He took this paper to the pharmacy along with $142.53 and in exchange was given a small plastic bottle of peach-colored pills, each octagonal in shape with the number 200 imprinted on one side. He swallowed one half-pill each morning with a mouthful of water. For the few seconds that the pill rested on his tongue, it tasted metallic, orange, sweet.

The literature warned him to expect nausea, insomnia, somnolence, back pain, fatigue, rash, rhinitis, abdominal pain, and xerostomia after taking the pills. And he experienced some of these at one moment or another. He also experienced a loss of appetite and a severe increase in irritability that tended to peak between 4 and 6 p.m. each day. He was also warned to watch for a skin rash that could be a symptom of toxic epidermal necrolysis and the potentially fatal Stevens-Johnson syndrome.

Shortly after he began the inhibition, he started going to a small room that had been made available to him by a local arts organization after he had submitted a three-page, double-spaced project proposal, his CV, and a budget proposal, on which he had simply written "$0."

Each day, he went to the room and put his body in a different position and then held it without moving for most of the day. The first day of his project found him in the small room, standing naked with his left leg crossed in front of his right leg, both hands held out to the side, palms up, head forward. He held this pose for six hours and then went home.

The next day he spent naked in the room, standing with his knees bent, his left knee slightly ahead of his right, his penis resting on top of his pressed together thighs, his hands in front of him, bent at the elbow, two fingers on one hand making a V sign.

The next day, he stood clothed and balanced on his left leg, his right foot out to the side, bent at the waist, his right arm as if pulling a sack down over a face, his torso bent.

The day after that he was clothed, squatting down, balanced on the front of his feet, his head forward and down, his spine straight and aligned, his right arm pulled back, right hand in a fist as if ready to punch a body on the floor.

The next day, he stood naked with his arms

spread out behind him, his upper torso bending backwards, his head held up and facing forward, a pair of women's underpants over his face.

There was no audience for what he did. There was no documentation. He never spoke about the project or about the room that the arts organization had loaned to him.

He left the room each day by 4 p.m. and walked home. Once home, he would walk the dogs. Once they had their walk, he would make himself a drink and begin what he called "working on his writing," which meant that he might check his email and various social network feeds, grade several student essays, make some lists, and then stare into space, grinding his teeth and listening to the ice cubes swirling in his glass.

After some days of taking the pills and going to the small room to do the project, his body began to smell stale and sour and his arms and shoulders began to go numb. They felt weak, or numb, or not weak or numb but something like weak or numb, something wrong, something wrong and yet without pain. It was as if his body was layering itself with woven or laminated fibers so as to spread the energy from the poses, bringing them to a stop before they could penetrate into him.

Still, he continued on.

The next day he spent his time in the small room clothed, standing with his legs spread apart as if straddling a dog, his arms bent at the elbows, his hands gripping as if holding the dog's chain, his torso bending forward as if over the dog, his head forward.

The day after that, he sat clothed with his legs bent at the knees and underneath him, his arms behind his back as if handcuffed, his torso leaning back, his face forward.

The next day, he was naked and on his back, his knees bent, his hands holding his head.

The next, he was clothed, his feet close together, his weight on his left leg, standing straight, his left arm bent and a little forward of his body, his right arm relaxed.

During his walk home one night, he became even more numb. Once home, after walking the dogs and making himself his drink and grading four and a half student essays, he lay down and passed out on the couch. He woke up with his shoulders frozen. He couldn't move his neck or hands. His body had moved beyond woven and laminated and it was as if it was now growing a metal exoskeleton of plates.

He spent the weekend on the couch, working on his writing, which that weekend took the form of writing sentences in his head. When he was able to raise himself up and off the couch, he began to carry his arms crab-like in front of him, his fingers together, one thumb held up.

On Monday, he pulled himself up and lurched to the small room to continue the project. On his way to the room, he stopped thinking of his arms as claws, even though as he walked he held his hands out in front of him, bent at the elbows, his fingers together, one thumb held up. That day, he lay on the floor on his left side, his hands behind his back as if hand-cuffed together, his underpants around his thighs, his left knee bent, his left foot underneath his right knee, his right foot at a ninety-degree angle.

The next day, he was clothed, standing, his feet slightly wider than his hips, resting his weight on his right leg, his right hand relaxed and hanging, his left hand outstretched as if holding a leash, his head turned to the left, bent slightly forward.

The day after that he spent standing, naked, a sack on his head, his left arm stretched out from his body, his right arm parallel with his shoulder, his elbow bent, his hand dropping, as if handcuffed to a wall.

The next day, he stood clothed, his legs spread a little wider than his waist, more weight on his left leg, both feet facing forward, his arms bent at the elbows, his hands as if holding a baton, his face forward.

All that week, whenever he was not working on his project in the small room, he lurched when he walked, one shoulder higher than the other, one leg dragging a little, and as he walked, he held his arms in front of him, bent at the elbows, his fingers together, one thumb up. Finally, by late Friday afternoon, he lurched into the welcoming, naturally lit office of a nearby specialist.

The specialist's name was Laura. She was healthy and fit. Her eyes creased reassuringly when she smiled. She also had an easy manner. She had a light touch, an interest in healing, and a faith in using alternative medicines to stimulate the body to cleanse all that the culture deposits or stirs up within. She began by touching his neck. She claimed on the basis of this touch that he had a virus that was causing his back and neck and shoulders and hands and fingers to seize up. I can tell from the way you are sweating, she told him. It smells metallic, sweet. She left the room and returned a few minutes later pushing a small metal tray. On the tray were bottles of supplements. She took each bottle off the tray and held it near his neck and then moved it slowly down the front of his body, holding his left arm up and pulling on it as he resisted, whispering to herself as she did this. Based on the resistance of his arm, she prescribed various herbal extracts and glands of mammals for him to ingest. She prescribed combinations of bovine adrenal gland, porcine brain tissue, bovine tissues from the hypothalamus, pituitary, and pineal glands, bovine and ovine spleen, bovine pancreas, liver, pituitary, kidney, prostate, and liver fat. These supplements had been collected from the wastes of slaughterhouses and then dried and packaged into multicolored gelatin capsules. Some of these he was to suck on so that the active components were absorbed by the tongue for rapid action with the brain. Some he was to swallow. Some came in suppository form that he would insert into his anus before bed. He presented her with $95 and in return received a sack full of supplements.

He again spent the weekend on the couch, working on his writing, which that weekend took the form of writing sentences in his head in between grading student essays, sipping his drink, and rubbing his dogs' ears whenever they wandered near.

The next week began with him back at the small room that the arts organization had loaned him. He spent the day in his underwear, evenly balanced on his legs, which he held a little wider than his hips, his feet forward, his torso bent, his arms as if tied behind his knees, his head bent at the neck and lifted.

His shoulders continued to seize. He continued to lurch along, dragging one leg. He could not tilt his head nor could he place his right hand over his forehead and rub the area of his forehead and eyes with a strong squeezing motion. When he graded student essays he could barely grip the pen and his marks became increasingly jagged and cartoon-like.

It was around this time that he doubled his dosage of the small peach pills that inhibited his voltage-sensitive sodium channels. He was now spending $5 a day blocking his sodium channels and around $3 a day on the crushed glands and adrenals of various mammals. Each morning he would count out all the pills, swallow some of them, mix others with water and squirt them in his mouth, and at night lodge still others in his anus.

The next day, back at the small room, while he was clothed, kneeling forward, his arms resting on his legs, his head lifted, he felt a tingling in his face. By the time he was done, the tingling had developed into what appeared to be a boil on his cheek.

He lurched home that day from his small room and, as he always did, he ate his dinner, graded three student essays, and walked the dogs. While he was walking the dogs that evening, he felt a liquid oozing down his face. When he got home and looked in the mirror, he realized that what he had thought was just a boil was something more. It had grown into eight soft blisters, all clustered together, at moments overlapping. His epidermis seemed to be separating from his dermis and the space created by this separation was filling up with a liquid consisting of dead and living cells that was whitish-yellow in color. This whitish-yellow liquid oozed out and then slowly dripped down his face. He grabbed some toilet paper and pressed down on the blisters to collect the fluid, as if it was possible to join the epidermis and the dermis back together just by pushing on them.

Thus began the period of time in which he worried about his face leaking, about the space between the dermis and the epidermis. It was not that this was a major ailment. It was not that it mattered really. It was more that his body was constantly and irritatingly reminding him of something, something that he would rather forget, but something that he was unable to forget because it had entered into his body and reshaped him. From then on, he spent a great deal of his days focused on this spot on his cheek, hyperaware of any sort of potential dripping. All day long, he pressed down on the blisters with small pieces of toilet paper, attempting to drain them, attempting to prevent them from dripping into his food or his drink or onto the student essays. All day long they would refill.

No one knew what caused the leakage or how to end it.

He called his doctor and joked to him that he was ill with late capitalism. His doctor did not laugh, just replied that he was to come in to the sterile, overly lit office if the blisters spread, and then reminded him that one possible side effect of his medication included a potentially fatal condition that would first present itself as clusters of blisters. He then thanked him for calling and said that he would receive a bill sometime next week.

A few days later, he made the same joke about being ill with late capitalism to the specialist. Laura, billing at a more reasonable rate, smiled a sad yet patient smile, touched his neck and asked to smell his breath. She replied that there was no such thing as capitalism and then prescribed a series of homeopathic laxatives. She said that his leaking face was evidence that his body was successfully cleansing itself of the virus, cleansing itself of numerous parasites, and the thing to do was to help it along. She again tested the strength of his arm while whispering to herself and holding various bottles over his kidneys and spleen, or just above his blisters, and from the response of his arm again prescribed a series of additional supplements. She swabbed his cheek with a tissue and told him she would do an energy reading of the tissue sample.

While Laura's laxatives helped him further cleanse, as she phrased it, not much else happened. His face continued to leak. He continued working on his project, spending a typical day lying naked on his left side on the floor, his knees bent up around his chest, his left hand out straight along the floor, his right hand in front of his chest, resting on the floor by his shoulder, his head lifted off the floor, pus dripping from his cheek and onto the floor.

Eventually the lurching and the dripping, the frozen shoulders and the claws, the cleansing and the clenching became too much and he decided to stop the project. Or perhaps he simply went home one day and didn't return the next. The ending of his project was uneventful. On the last day, he lay on his side on the floor naked, his knees slightly bent, his torso bent at the waist, his left arm out straight and held up as if it were resting on the body of someone who was on the floor next to him. Whitish-yellow liquid slowly dripped across his face and collected in a small puddle on the floor. When he was done lying on the floor, he got up, cleaned up the puddle with a mop, put the mop back in its bucket, and then walked home. His face continued to seep. He continued to press a small piece of toilet paper against it.

He began to spend most of his days at home, working on his writing, which included grading papers, drinking, taking his pills and inserting his suppositories, swabbing his leaking blisters, going to the bathroom to shit or get more toilet paper. He tried to write about his project in the small room and then tried not to write about the project and then not to think about the project. He spent hours on the Internet, clicking on an article about Courbet and then editing the Wikipedia entry on the Vendôme Column, reading a feminist critique of dirty realism, an article about yet another bombing in Tikrit, then checking the online map application that marked each new occupation of a public space as it happened, then watching again and again the video that showed a woman in Russia going into a grocery store, removing her panties, sticking a whole uncooked chicken up her cunt, and then walking out of the store to later cook the chicken for her friends and collaborators. Then he tried to not think about how not thinking or not writing about the project might be why he was now only able to pull himself back and forth from the couch to the toilet, leaking and lurching, as if the

exoskeleton on his shoulders and back and his fes-
tering blisters would not let him forget, but instead
would require even more cleansing.

And so one night, still leaking and shitting from
the supplement-induced cleansing, he lurched to the
couch and, one by one, dragged each cushion and pil-
low and blanket and dog bed and throw rug and soft
sculpture and roll of toilet paper and tossed them
down the stairs into the basement. Then he lowered
himself down the stairs and into the dank softness.
The basement was cool and moist, messy and moldy.
At first, he just lay there befuddled, trying to relax
and breathe into the soft site he'd made with the pil-
lows and the cushions.

Eventually he pulled himself up and decided
that to further cleanse himself he would clean out
the mess of the basement. He began by throwing
out parking tickets from cars he no longer owned,
postcards for art shows he could barely remember,
years of mortgage statements and cancelled checks,
old unread magazines that had material in them
that he thought he might use at some point for
a journal that he no longer edited. He threw out
photocopies of scholarly articles, many of them unread, that he had collected as research from graduate seminars he had attended, an old thesis he had

written about the political economy of Zimbabwe, an essay he had written about Providence that was called "City of Plastic Jewels," letters from friends he had made while he had lived in Harare, articles he had used while attempting to write on literature's role in national resistance movements, and vinyl 45s of his college band, the Omar Saeed Quintet, playing "Pants-down in the Rise-up." He threw out 278 graded essays that former students had never retrieved. He threw out a moldy copy of Raymond Carver's selected stories and old scores to songs he'd composed when he first moved to San Francisco. He threw out poems from a writing workshop he'd started at a homeless shelter years ago. He threw out photographs from an old relationship, photographs whose power he attempted to hold at bay by thinking of them as only poses, photographs that showed him holding hands with a woman that he had deeply loved on a trip to Italy or a photo of both of them, their arms around each other, holding the puppy they'd adopted, or the two of them at an antiwar march just before they broke up. He threw out what he thought of as the divorce agreement from this relationship, even though they'd never been married. He threw out a love letter from someone whose signature and handwriting he could not recognize. All of this he placed in paper bags and then put out in front of his house to be recycled.

After that, he began to spend more and more time in the basement, among the remaining boxes and papers, the moldy books and the moldy drywall. His cheek continued to fill with whitish-yellow liquid and this whitish-yellow liquid continued to leak down his face and he continued to press a small piece of toilet paper onto his face, drawing and collecting the whitish-yellow liquid, and then he once again began what he thought of as working on his writing, often sleeping in a net that hung from the exposed sewage pipes, pipes that transferred his waste through the basement and out into the system that collected it along with everyone else's in his city and the neighboring city to the north. The net was a sculpture that he'd purchased at a fundraiser for a small nonprofit arts organization, a sculpture titled "Support Network." He would hoist himself up into it and sag into the pose of a hibernating panda, or at other times, he would sleep curled up on a piece of drywall placed across two sawhorses, pressing his face against the drywall to swab and collect the whitish-yellow liquid, the drywall filling up with the liquid of dead and living cells, in turn producing parasites and mold spores and an odor of sweet, metallic, musty gin. He mentally registered the drywall in the basement sagging and seeping, the phrase "the basement" reminding him of the word "debasement," and he felt stupid for thinking that such semblances might mean anything, for imagining that puns might provide a provisional solution to an impasse, or might allow one's sense of one's life to sag with stupid metaphors, since metaphors are for books and not for actual people.

Eventually the swabbing and the shitting, the mold spores and the smell of the basement became too much and he decided to leave the basement, to find some other kind of cleansing or treatment for all the symptoms of his actions and inactions. Or perhaps he simply went upstairs one day and didn't return the next and instead went over to his friend's house.

Once there, he helped her make a soup that they decided to think of as a spell, a spell that might clear the effects of the cleansing they'd each been doing separately but together, a spell that might bring out the writing that might lead them to some action that they hoped was stuck inside their bodies. The soup was to be composed half of vegetables grown below ground and half of vegetables grown above ground. Their soup included carrots, onions, beets, kale, celery, zucchini, salt, rosemary, and water. Together they chopped and they minced and, before they put the soup on the stove to steam and stew, they each spat into the pot for good measure. Once the soup was on, they brought out the ice bucket and the gin and talked about their projects and their impasses and their failures and frustrations. They talked about friendship, about their friendships with others, about the moments when friendship gets complicated by gender and sexuality, layered with social and institutional frames of power, cultural capital, competition, gossip, know-it-ism, scolding, gate-keeping, team-building, inappropriate touching, scene policing, after-parties, and yet at the same time could be fortified and fed by something as simple as making soup together.

They sat down at the table to eat their soup. They sipped their soup and wiped their lips and chins and thought about soup making. Could soup be an aesthetic object that might tell them something about relations between people and the world? Could it be a model of possible universes, a way they might learn how to inhabit the world in a better way? Or could it be just soup, nurturing and warm in the belly? They banged their metal spoons on the table, and they talked about how the table was and was not a metaphor. Could the table be an object of labor that tells them something about relations between people and the world? Obviously they couldn't make the table talk or dance or eat grass. But perhaps they could press against it until they believed they were feeling the sensuous touch of whoever built it. Or they could sit around it like this, drinking and talking and sipping and slurping, with or without the proper political thinking or a clear plan for action, but in some kind of soup-eating solidarity and sense of greater purpose, in some semblance of the struggle-force they wanted bubbling in their soup and boiling in their guts.

They finished the soup and they relaxed into their chairs, their bellies full. The cat came prancing in from the backyard and scampered beneath the table. A light breeze blew in from the open back door. The sun was setting and it filled the room with the last of its yellow light. He took a sip from his drink, sighed, and then asked his friend, "Why do you think I'm so miserable?"

When she replied she did not mention the obvious. How late capitalism leaked out of his face. Or how alternative medicine's unregulated glands and adrenals of mammals collected from the waste of slaughterhouses leaked. Or how the pharmaceutical industry leaked. Or having no health insurance leaked. Or how the gratuitous torture that was done in their name leaked. Or now the various endless wars leaked. Or how what they meant by working on their writing leaked all of these things together but not in a way that they could yet recognize as their writing or their art.

Instead she paused, got up from the table and left her soup. She came back carrying a book and read a poem from it:

I wandered lonely as a cloud
That floats on high o'er vales and hills,
When all at once I saw a crowd,
A host, of golden daffodils;
Beside the lake, beneath the trees,
Fluttering and dancing in the breeze.

Continuous as the stars that shine
And twinkle on the Milky Way,
They stretched in never-ending line
Along the margin of a bay:
Ten thousand saw I at a glance,
Tossing their heads in sprightly dance.

The waves beside them danced; but they
Out-did the sparkling waves in glee:
A poet could not but be gay,

In such a jocund company:
I gazed—and gazed—but little thought
What wealth the show to me had brought:

For oft, when on my couch I lie
In vacant or in pensive mood,
They flash upon that inward eye
Which is the bliss of solitude;
And then my heart with pleasure fills,
And dances with the daffodils.

He lifted his drink, swirling the ice cubes in his
glass with his finger. He tilted his head, slumped his
shoulders, placed his right hand over his forehead,
and rubbed the area of his forehead and eyes with
a strong squeezing motion, making a not-quite-
exasperated-yet-thinking-hard-about-it-but-also-
frustrated face.

When he got home later that night, he poured himself a drink, sat down at his kitchen table, and began
to write. What he had meant to write was a description of the project that he had done in the small room.
How each day he had held the pose of a person who
was torturing someone or who was being tortured by
someone. His source for each pose had been a series

of photographs that had been found on the Internet, photographs taken in an overseas military prison called "The Hard Site." As he re-created the poses he had not distinguished between who tortured and who was tortured. He had let both shape his body. What he had meant to write was about his decision to do this project, to put his body into the position of particular others, that indexical other without whom no one can know one's own self. About his attempt to think of his life as part of a series of complex, passion-ate, antagonistic, and necessary relations to others who act and are acted upon. But it kept going wrong. In the writing he could not do, he was trying to de-scribe something that might be artful, might have something to say about the political moment, and yet could live safely in a room loaned out to him by an arts organization dedicated to the parsing out of aes-thetic experiences to a demographically appropriate audience for a nominal cover charge. But he was also attempting to think about how his passivity contrib-uted to all this, how even doing nothing might have seemed the opposite of contributing. About his reser-vations around this project, this different kind of con-tribution, about its relationship to a mortifying and paralyzing shame, about its ineffectiveness. About the limits of art done in isolation. About the limits of art.

He wrote in the third person. Then he wrote in the first person. He wrote from a male point of view and then from a female point of view. He wrote himself into the piece. He wrote himself out of the piece. He wanted to title what he wrote "The Remedy," but he was not sure there could be a remedy for what ailed him, at least not as art or writing. He soldiered on through the night, until sunlight began to creep through the kitchen windows and the dogs began to wake, stretch, and rub against his legs. He heard the day's first train rumble along the raised subway line two blocks over. He raised himself up from the table, called the still sleepy dogs to him and, rubbing their ears softly, began to read to them what he had written.

"After I had the baby," he read, "I was often desperate to get out of the house, to walk somewhere and be near other people. Even though I was always with the baby," he said, "I felt very much as if I was by myself. So to be near other people I would go for long walks, carrying the baby in a sack that hung from my shoulder. On these walks, I would be near other people only for a few brief moments as I passed them by. Still, that felt like it was some sort of more to me," he said. "On these walks, if the baby started to cry I would stop and sit on a nearby bench and nurse him. Sometimes men spat at me as I did this. At first,

I was not accustomed to being spat upon and when it happened I would be surprised and dismayed. But eventually I got used to it and came to expect it.

"I got used to the spitting," he said, "but I did not get used to having the body that got spat upon. My mind would think something about how my body is once again my body. But my body was not really agreeing with this because it felt even less like it was mine. When the baby came out," he told the dogs, "something that was not me left me. However, it had not left me with my former self but rather with a new self, and I did not yet feel as if this new self was mine. My body did new and often unexpected things. It was not just that my breasts now produced milk and the milk seemed to have a life of its own, spurting out across the room at times. And it was not just that new hormones coursed through my body and made me feel new emotions, some pleasant and some not. But my brain was also different. And so when I tried to talk about my new self, the new self that did not yet feel as if it was mine, or talk from this new self, I did not know the right language. The new self's language seemed to have a life of its own, spurting out at times. Words and expressions came out wrong. Often I said them backwards or I confused their order in sentences. Or I would try to say I feel weird and I would find myself saying I am fat. Or I would try to say I love you and I would find myself saying I hate you. Or I would want to say poetry matters and I would instead find myself saying poetry is a waste of time."

The dogs scratched their bellies with their hind legs, got up and wandered over to their food and water bowls, did the usual things that dogs do, but he continued reading to them.

"Not only did I not know the right language," he said, "I didn't really know how to fuck anymore. Nursing would send oxytocin coursing through my body, so I knew how my body might feel good. But I could no longer remember how to make oxytocin when fucking, although I did remember that fucking should make oxytocin. After the baby came out, there was a hole in my body and I had not yet figured out how to fill it. When I had sex at first, the hole felt big, too big. The baby had only stretched a hole for a few minutes as he descended down and out of my birth canal, but it was long enough to stretch it out, and it took several months for it to close back up. When I fucked someone now, there might at moments be something inside that hole, something filling it up, but I was still not whole.

"A few months after the baby was born," he continued, "after I started fucking again, I began to spit on my lovers, usually when we were fucking. Even though by this time I was used to men spitting on me when I nursed, my sudden desire to spit on my lovers was unexpected. I did not know what to make of it. Sometimes my lovers would, exasperated, scream at me to stop spitting. But most of the time we just kept fucking, my lovers sometimes dodging the spit, sometimes just lying there and putting up with it.

"Soon after I started spitting on my lovers, I started doing sit-ups. I did three sets of thirty each day. I began to masturbate regularly again. And I returned to work. My first week back at work I began importing submachine guns to Guinea through an Egyptian arms broker named Sharif al-Masri. And also I began to collaborate with a friend on a piece of writing about a small historically unimportant plot of land. I did all of this with a hole in me. I often started my day by attempting to fill the hole by fucking my lovers. I often did three sets of thirty sit-ups while my lovers gave the baby breakfast. I tended to masturbate later in the day. Part of most days were spent thinking about the collaboration. My collaborator and I would often give each other assignments and usually neither of us did them, so I usually just thought about the collaboration rather than doing it. Then often I made some phone calls to see if the weapons had arrived yet. If they had arrived some-place, like say Uganda, I would claim that they did not meet specifications in the contract and request that al-Masri return them to the manufacturer."

He paused, took a deep breath, and exhaled. "Day after day went like this. One day I would sell the arms to Pecos, a Guinean brokering company later linked to a series of illicit arms transfers to Liberia instead of arranging for them to be shipped back to Slovakia. Another day, after I was done masturbating, I might see about the delivery of one thousand submachine guns to Liberia along two parallel tracks, one origi-nating in Moldova and the other in Liberia. Then I would divert submachine guns to Guinea through an elaborate bait-and-switch scheme that spanned three continents. And at the same time, I would con-tinue to think about how to make collaborative art and suggest to my collaborator that we make a lyrical poem and how in this poem there could be a list of all the cars that drove by the small plot of land over a span of ten minutes and how much gas was being consumed by cars as they drove by the small plot of land and that perhaps this poem would then be about both the bourgeois individualism of the lyric and the extremities of consumption that define us. And while thinking about the poem, I would masturbate with a brown medium-size dildo and think about my lovers or sometimes the breasts of a younger woman and then when I came I might say one of my lovers' names or I might say 'fuck.' Later that day, my collaborator would email me and suggest for our collaboration that he put an ad on an Internet website that said he would be at the small historically unimportant plot of land for six hours one day with a set of nunchucks and that anyone who wanted to come by and beat him up was welcome to do so and perhaps this would be about a rejection of his white and Western and patriarchal privilege. I would then seek and receive permission in Moldova to charter an Ilyushin airliner to another Moldovan company, MoldTransavia, and claim that the aircraft was needed as a substitute for a damaged Tupolev-154 originally scheduled to fly passengers from the UAE to Moldova. I would do another thirty sit-ups, working on keeping my neck relaxed at the same time. And then when the arms arrived in the UAE I would call and say that the Tu-154 had been repaired and had already flown back to Moldova with its passengers and then I would get a representative of Centrafrican Airlines, Serguei Denissenko, to give me a new contract to fly cargo, identified as 'Technical Equipment,' to Uganda and then on to Liberia. When one of my lovers was inside of me, I would think at that moment about the hole in my body or I would imagine that I had my lovers in my chest. And after I had signed the contract and faxed it back the Il-18 would depart for Uganda. And while it flew to Uganda, I would meet my collaborator on the small historically unimportant plot of land with a few sprigs of rosemary and we would rub some of the rosemary between our fingers and sniff deeply the rosemary smells on our fingers and imagine we were the opposite of our individual genders and then we would sit down in the grass on the small plot of land and write furiously from this position. And whatever my gender was at that moment, later that night when we fucked, one of my lovers would begin by putting thumbs on my nipples and cupping my breasts and while fucking, my breasts would leak milk and then the ants would begin to gather in our bed, attracted by the milk. After we fucked, and usually before the ants figured out that there was milk in the bed, I would get up and sign another charter contract for the Il-18 with Centrafrican. While I signed the charter, I would imagine we had a different body, a different societal gender conditioning. And from this different societal gender conditioning, I would teach my lovers about my hole, the hole that my lovers kept trying to fill by sticking stuff in it."

The dogs had moved to the door and were looking back at him with wagging tails and what he thought might be impatient faces, but he continued reading. "Often, after we fucked, I would read to one of my lovers the charter contract, which listed a cargo of 14.5 tons, the exact weight if the plane had flown the full amount of rifles to Liberia in two separate flights, and the same routing specified in the contract with Vichi. Meanwhile, we would attempt to get inside some other skin. And I would show my lovers how to put a different sort of pressure on the fleshy area right behind the front of the entrance to my hole, which the contract referred to as 'the performance of several air transportations,' the same name we chose for our other skin, in our other genders. I would show my lovers how to use not only back-and-forth pressure but also side-to-side and as my lovers did this, shortly after the Ilyushin arrived in Entebbe, and loaded my breasts with seven tons of sealed boxes containing one thousand of the 2,250 submachine guns that the Ugandan government believed were being returned to the manufacturer in Slovakia, my collaborator and I would be able to think together about how our writing could be different, all the things it wouldn't be, or shouldn't be, how our bodies might be different, our holes, our thoughts, our desires, with additional arms transfers procuring collaboration and the sweat pouring out of us, with requisite pressure on the fleshy areas, someone's leg twitching, bent over at ninety degrees with head thrown back, all who are there in whatever genders breathing heavy and quick. And sometimes I would, say, go around the entire lip of the hole, as the plane headed west and arrived in Monrovia on November 22nd, and as we landed we would sniff the herbs on our fingers while thinking and writing from our other skin, our other genders, our other holes, our other poses, our other others, all in adjacency, to the guns and the cars and the plot of land at the border between our cities, and to our lovers and our fleshy areas and our dildos, and to our leaking drill-holes and our leaking breasts and our overripe insecurities, and to our stories, our biographies, our writing. And perhaps from this we could then build a bottom-up, participatory structure of society and culture, a two- and three- and more-way affair, about erect and sucking participation. With or without me, with or without my permission. For motherhood and fucking exist as necessary paradigms of creation, ones where anyone can be an artist-lover and anyone can succeed. And through all of this I will continue to contribute, to bend and to leak, to adapt and mutate, adding yet more ingredients that we do not own to things that are beautiful, revolutionary, and irretrievable."

He stopped reading. The dogs were now whimpering, pawing at the door to go out. He sent the file to the printer and then took the warm freshly printed pages down into the basement and filed them in a cardboard box labeled "treatments." He lifted the box up on to the makeshift sawhorse table and returned upstairs. He put some doggie bags into the right rear pocket of his jeans and some toilet paper into the left rear pocket, then put the leashes on the dogs, opened the door, and walked upright out into the sweet, crisp morning air.

AN ARMY OF LOVERS

THE NEXT DAY, KOKI and Demented Panda returned to the small plot of land. They sat together in the smoldering ash and raw sewage that their spells and spills and flesh-guns had brought about, surveying the wreckage. They had walked to the small plot of land from their homes in their two different cities to be together, not together in their separateness, but together, really together.

They had first come to the small plot of land so as to feel the collective possibility of two people coming together and writing with one hand. And they came to it now with the same desire, even though they had ongoing trouble in their coming together. Their collaboration was clearly not working and had not been working from the very beginning.

They had fought a lot about this, how to get themselves out of what they had taken to calling "the impasse," which was their inability to figure out why they continued to write poetry in a time when poetry seemed not to matter, and why their attempts to collaborate with one or maybe two or maybe four hands in order to break through this impasse continued to fail. They had said to each other that they didn't want to write any more poems that demonstrated their adept use of irony and book-smarts to communicate their knowing superiority to capitalism. And they didn't want to write any more poems that narrated their pseudo-edgy sexual exploits in a way to suggest that such exploits were somehow in and of themselves political. And they didn't want to write any more poems that made people feel sad or guilty or go "oh no." But still, it was hard for them to figure out what to do with poetry in a time when 24.5 acres were required to sustain their first-world lifestyles, not to mention that within the 24.5 acres were the deaths and devastation from the mining, oil, natural gas, and nuclear industries, the deaths and torture from the policies of their government, the rising acidity of the ocean, the effects of climate change on populations without access to the equivalent of 24.5 acres of resources. And rather than provoking in them the desire to write more poems, this sense of futility, further aggravating their anger and shame, instead infected them, manifesting in all variety of ailments and symptoms. As a result, they would often begin to tremble and shake, minuscule tremors rippling out from their enteric nervous systems and through the fibers of their organ-meat, coursing through their bloodstream and their compromised immune systems and out into the world beyond their bodies, the pent-up frustration and rage slowly seeping out of them, awkwardly, publicly, ineffectually.

So there they were, back on the small plot of land, and they decided that as card-carrying Bay Area poets they would of course attempt to enter into a trance state together and through this trance they hoped they might move from the places of worry and over-thinking in their birdbrains and panda-heads to some kind of right proper political thinking and feeling and action, to move beyond the many impasses that so defined them, defined their relationships with others, defined their lives as poets.

They had brought their yoga mats with them and so they lay down on their mats and closed their eyes and breathed in all that was there, the smoky air, the charred plastics and the metals, the sewage and the stink, but also the faint smells of rosemary and the wet sidewalk and the sweet, metallic gasoline fumes, all of it there in the soft breeze that ever-so-lightly tickled the hairs on Demented Panda's paws and ever-so-gently ruffled Koki's feathers. As they lay there, eyes closed, together and yet not touching, they heard the cars continue to drive by, the heavy-rail public rapid transit system careening through the tunnel, the people continuing to walk by on their way to more hospitable places, pushing strollers or walking their dogs or talking on their cellphones. There on their yoga mats, Demented Panda and Koki took deep breaths and felt their breastplates rising and falling as they relaxed their bodies into the ground. And with each breath, they dropped into being relaxed, bright, and natural, dropped into being with the small plot of land, with its still smoldering trash and rot as well as its regenerative energies and resilient ecologies. As they became increasingly relaxed, bright, and natural, they counted the cars as they heard them drive by, not simply as bits of data but as bodily-felt. And they heard the high-pitched screeching of the heavy-rail public rapid transit system careening along the overpass, not as a source of anxiety but as something simply there, a melodic fact that made their arms and legs become even more relaxed. And they tuned into each person as they walked by, noticing how all of them were breathing in and out just as they were breathing in and out. And eventually they began to think about how they were a part of the cars and the heavy-rail public rapid transit system and the people walking by and the kids in strollers and dogs on leashes and people on the other sides of the cellphone conversations that moved through electromagnetic radiation in the microwave range to and from signal towers and satellites orbiting the planet as much as they were a part of themselves and of each other.

And though they also knew burning, knew crumpled bags of Frito-Lay corn chips drifting through the air, knew sacks pulled out of one's pants or pulled down over one's head, knew bending their torsos at ninety-degree angles, knew holding out their arms to be strength-tested, and though they also knew desire, raw and furious, knew how to put one finger in the cold gin and swirl the ice cubes while putting another finger in the warm soup to check for taste while using yet one more finger to rub vigorously back and forth and then push send, right then all they needed to know was this breathing. And though they could feel resistance and skepticism and doubt inside themselves as they thought about their collaboration and how much of it was done in isolation from some greater collective purpose, or how it often seemed so focused on the I, I, I of their individual selves and their self-styled pseudo-heroic lifestyles, seemed so focused on the I, I, I of yet more autobiography, memoir, bourgeois individualist lyricism, and North American navel-gazing, and though their shame and embarrassment at this threatened to only re-fortify the impasses they'd pledged to overcome, right then all they needed to know was this breathing.

And then, with the utmost mindfulness, they stood up and brushed themselves off, still breathing deeply, feeling now bright and fevered for ever-broader interactions and exchanges, ever-more-lateral routes to touching and adjacency, as if attached by cephalopod suckers to each other, and ready now to move through the world with a tenfold increase in interest in it.

So they turned to each other in their trance state and to each other that was not them, in whatever bodies or genders they had at that moment, and with feet spread slightly wider than their shoulders and pressed firmly into the ground, nostrils flaring and upper lips slightly snarled, they breathed even more deeply and proclaimed, to each other and to each other's others and to all the willing monsters, to the friends and lovers and ex-lovers and frenemies, some at the bar and some at the staff meeting, some in the streets and some on the organizing committees, to the crooked and the bent, the oversexed and the underemployed, to the gin-soaked cynics and the beautiful losers, to the viruses and the parasites thriving within them, and with ever-growing intensity to the gathering hive buzzing there now amidst the glitter and ash, they spoke as one and declared, with tenfold determination together and to each other, let us come together now, let's now let's, let's call out the animal inside us that bucks for peace and fucking, and then let's brandish our pirate flags and set to it. Let's clear the fields of all that hinders and hounds us, declare all contracts made in our name but without our consent null and void, and then charter illicit transport for all those who crave elsewhere and otherwise. What comes out of you or me comes out of all of us, which is why we want to dance with you in the common sluice without shame or hesitation, for we have wasps planted in us and want together to grow monstrous side branches that topple the stalks of you and us, so we might together bend the sound of poems and anti-poems beyond the fenced horizon, and so to those who've yet to join us we sing out, hold high your bandaged wrists and ankles and we will show you our boils and blisters, in sympathy and solidarity, in mutual recognition and misrecognition and in mutating symbiosis. And those who we've yet to join, that larger us that we hope will gather two mediocre yet willing poets into its folds, we hope that you sing back to us, c'mon feel the noise, so that our chakras might resonate in the often fraught and contradictory yet purposeful ache of our numbers, and so that in return we can hold high our saddle-stitched chapbooks and show you our imitation-leather chaps, made from the repurposed vinyl of a thousand punk rock LPs, framing our beatific multigenerational and diversely gravitational asses for consensual fondling or tickling or playful spanking. And from this call and response we will find ourselves abuzz with a potency that fills the air with the scent of sex and rutting, of skin-sap and untold side effects. For look, there are bears on the balconies, lapping honey off the rims of their whiskey glasses, so let's raise our paws and wings and whoop and whistle freely with them until those more attuned to the tremors within our collective flesh-heat begin to feverishly exclaim, here come the horses, horses, horses, so let's go out to get the giddy-up, go out and meet the push-back with the head-on fortitude of the you and the we in this growing us, with nothing but poems and lust on our lips, declaring passion, fury, and fight. And we will insist that these poems, those that pun on the word capitalism and those that proclaim domestic love as labor worth slant-rhyming for, those that seem to celebrate with whatever degree of irony our daily lives and lacks, and those that value the kinds of prosodic craft that one can only be trained in at the pricey Master of Flatulent Arts programs, those that construct elaborate socio-political walls to bang one's head against, gathering the resulting splinters and sparks into fragmented sound poems, and those that collect the thick idiolects of Internet culture and from this compost heap harvest uncanny confession-alisms, we will take these and all other poems inside us, by tearing them into a thousand tiny shreds and then eating those shreds and shitting them out and then from our excrement making new poems or anti-poems. Even as we speak, we are pouring the whis-keys with which to wash down the cut-ups while we prepare ourselves to receive the resultant riches from your lovely assholes, regardless of age or cleanliness, since as we love you all we are ready to get down in it, for the pleasures to be found in the rich heady aro-mas of shit and poetry and love are the pleasures that will fuel any revolt worth getting down on our knees for. And if you'd rather take the poems and with them roll joints filled with medicinal marijuana and other herbal remedies, then we will commence with baking fair-trade vegan munchies whilst reminding the legume-intolerant among us to beware the soy-based inks used to print our poems on the 100%

recycled post-consumer waste paper, 'cuz that's how we roll. At the very least we will be happy soldiers to know that poetry might yet have helped nourish entire regiments of lovers, with poems in the lungs and the guts, knowing that at least in the bodies of those of us willing to masticate and swallow, inhale and ingest, somehow poetry will have mattered. And if a fungus appears, we will feed it freshly cut plant material and keep it free from mold and then make special structures that we might call gongylidia and upon these cultivate a bacterium that grows on us and grows on you and secretes chemicals that will seep out of our pores and holes, which we will then collect in small tinctures to use as preemptive remedies against the coming crackdowns. And yes, the crackdowns are coming, and as we've wet our whistles and tuned our chakras and written the showtunes, let's get on with goddamn show. And when they send in the wolves, we will join the wolves and return with teeth sharper and blood hotter. And when they slice off our tentacles, we will mutate, each sucker writhing outward in all directions. And then after we grow another tentacle, and cultivate yet more fungus, do not doubt for a moment that we will join the colts and blend in with the galloping menagerie of you horses and riders, you poets and pirates, you masked brigades and brass-band misfits, you feral cats and you feral grad students. So let's put to it and clear the streets of cars and billboards and ATMs and past-due bill notices, discovering in every intersection a dance floor, pulsing with unleashed beats and feedback loops of crooked laughter, in harmony or disharmony, from each according to their skillz and to each according to their booty. All this with hunger in our hips, such palpable lust not for bodies but for togetherness and for whatever might yet quiver beyond the law. And if we need to stop and catch our breath because, comrades, some of us are creaky in the knees and cranky in the brain-meat and riddled with energy-sucking viruses and shy to be seen experiencing even a brief moment of shame-free and seemingly directionless joy, even then, as we taste the doubt and cynicism creeping up the back of our dried-out throats, we hope there will be strangers among us who will still, despite our bad breath and our sagging bellies, our genital cheese and graying pubes, touch us lightly from behind and then turn us around and kiss us passionately but without imposition, with or without eye contact, the saliva on your tongues transmitting surplus electrolytes and pheromones, recharging us for the fight. For when they pen us in the enclosures, we will need to have already become a coven of women, a coven that includes those with penises and those with cunts and those with both, who will have begun to dismantle the blockades and the fences, salvaging the metals to later melt into slugs to get into the public pay-toilets, because while what women working together can accomplish is unlimited, our bladders are not, and pants-down in the rise-up isn't only for sexy-time. And through all of this we will have been holding hands together even though we might realize we are doomed to have failed for many centuries to come, still we want to come together and do this, again and again, just as, yes, we might write again and again another poem full of depressing statistics and anarchist one-liners. And when we see the yellow-sick wastewater leaking through the cracks and holes in the reinforced concrete bunker walls, we will stick out our thumbs not to plug the holes but to use our talon claws, freshly manicured in worker-owned avant-garde salons, to scrape and tear at the cracks, screeching in fake-witch voices, let it come down, let it come down. Thusly woman-identified, with numbers at the ready, we will collect the overflow and after using it to freshen our slits and creases, toiling and troubling, we will agitate and spit it back, boiling and bubbling. And we will share the pain when it comes, for it will come, even as it comes unevenly and more forcefully upon some more than others. And let this so-called brain disorder they want to cure us of, the one that provokes us to hit authority figures and show up late for meetings, multiply in our mucous membranes and from there pass through each writhing sucker, spitting ink and oozing cold jelly, nerve-charged contact jam spread all over our hot buns of steely resolve, working our core strength at the ice rink and saying to one another, dayum, let's hook up and overthrow the government. And then, reeking of sex and machine-grease, sweet and metallic, we will wipe our hands over the sweat-stained yoga mats and make of our fluids and your skin and your fluids and our skin the most powerful of potions, the musk of multitudes, and with our tongues in your armpits or lightly touching your backs we will push onward, chanting this is what poetry looks like, this is what poetry feels like, this is what poetry smells like. For we want to take all the forms and whimsies and all the meters and stanzas and all the calls for revolution and love and gargle and spit them and as we spit let us likewise secrete a mucus from tiny glands on our back that will feed the bacteria from the fungus and from that make a fleece-like covering on our backs to provide us a degree of insulation so we can rest our tail end near the hydrothermal vents of their thoughts, which spurt out at 176 degrees. And yes, we very well might have gas, nausea, and vomiting, we might be shaking the entire time, we might have concentration problems, joint pain, loss of appetite, neck pain, sinus infection, and sensitivity to the sun, might have nipple discharge, breast swelling, or primary malignant breast neoplasm, and yes we might have an increased incidence of malformation, such as a short tail or short body or vertebral disorganization, and yes, we might display bizarre behavior, agitation, or depersonalization, and complex behaviors such as sleep-driving after ingestion of a sedative-hypnotic, and yes, we might very well later find ourselves renally excreting sixty percent of the struggle together, with the additional forty percent excreted in our feces. But nonetheless, despite such side effects and the constant struggles to overcome them, do not doubt for a moment that we will stick chickens in our cunts with you and walk without hesitation or shame out of 24-hour grocery stores to the concrete parking lots where we will all eat together with friends and children and the grocery store baggers and all the stray animals drawn by the scent of liberated meat marinated in the sweet tang of pirate pussy, even as the vegetarians among us might playfully admonish the cunt-basters and chicken-tasters by applying parking lot weed garnishes to our ears and buttocks and overturning grocery carts upon themselves to perform agit-prop street theater reenactments of the conditions at industrial poultry farms. And if meanwhile we allow ourselves to be seduced into separating ourselves from each other via a thousand distractions and enticements, remind us to continue to travel together in a cloud as if we are the companions of the always moving shark, and let us suck against shark skin and eat shark feces. And if they try to appropriate and monetize forms of knowledge from us, the trans-species-companionship and herbal cures and homegrown kombucha and hypnotherapy scripts and the passwords to online membership in the Radical Riot Porn collective and our favorite pharmaceutical cocktail recipes, they will have to come take them from the small sacks hidden beneath the uniforms they make us wear, the dresses, the petticoats, the stockings, the girdles, the garters, the Spanx, the four-inch heels that push out our butts and jut out our breasts. And when they have offered us free downloads of movies in which characters are unable to connect because they are too depressed and their depression makes them unable to share anything with anyone, then despite the fact that some of us might find ourselves humming along with the demographically appropriate soundtrack of such entertainments, we want to remember that we can get up and wander out and instead lend our energies to the gigantic productions being rehearsed right outside our windows, preenactments of general strikes yet to come, with hundreds of thousands of participants who refuse to pay for art and refuse to be paid for art but still demand to make and experience art, and let us make of the collective labor and solidarity that will have to have been sweated out in the often and inevitably disharmonious entanglements a model for revolutionary methods of falling in love. And when they tell us to just calm down and have a good time, let us surprise even ourselves as we enjoy our guilt and complicity so much that as we cum we whisper into your ears our astronomical resource usage statistics, 24.5 acres, 24.5 acres, 24.5 acres. Let this fucking happen not just in the man-and-woman doggy style used in the "Fuck for the heir Puppy Bear!" action but also in the various woman-and-woman and man-and-man styles and trans-and-man and trans-and-woman styles and trans-and-trans styles and also in numerous other combinations, such as the Lucky Pierre–style so beloved by poets thanks to Frank O'Hara. And let us do this with you free of harassment and gender normative narratives so that if you say no, I prefer not to, we will listen, and if we say no, we prefer not to, we will listen, just as if you say let this arousal lead us to the new techniques we will also listen and if all are game we will writhe furiously from these positions. And we will have no numbers-trouble regarding the equitable distribution of orgasms among all the genders and all the critters, while at the same time reminding each other with our actions and our attentions that while our orgasms may be robust and bountiful we will feel equally loved and replenished by acts of care, wit, and the soft caressing of skin and pelt, just as we will have to have found new words for cumming as we rewire our erogenous circuits such that we find sexual bliss with works of art. That's right, we want art that makes us wet and driven, driven to flail and whelp and court failure in our impulse to action, again and again, failing with ever more grace and cunning, until futility becomes the magic that when dissolved beneath the tongue of all those ready to bark leads to ever more fruitful inquiries, for our bodies are bored by answers, which is why we wish to striate and rejuvenate the questions, even if in our questioning some of us are led to then ask how might we refuse this, refuse all of this. But know that we will be there with you, still, with your refusal, with our refusal. And if your refusal demands seemingly senseless acts of art, we will rush to the nearest public plazas and help turn over the police cars out front, rocking them with a back-and-forth motion and then when they are overturned we will mount them and simulate parodic acts of love-making with you, doing this together because it takes five or six, lovers or not, to overturn a police car, sometimes seven if its tank is still full of not-yet-ignited gasoline distilled from the finest international oil. Regardless, such acts can't be done alone or in isolation, just as it is often difficult to pull the needles out alone or in isolation or to build a giant worker-run counter-factory made of Legos amidst the roller coaster and other giant amusement rides in the central court of the Mall of America, fitting plastic piece into plastic piece in order to construct a gigantic Constructivist fantasia of interlocking reds and blacks, within which artists and lovers can hide in plain sight, stealing power from the Gap on the second floor and using crumbs from the food court to feed the hopeful monsters training for what will have become a new breed of revolutionary love-making mall rats, fueled by Orange Julius and the hive-buzz of fluorescent lighting, scurrying into the night armed with erect and pulsing genitalia and brains on permanent holiday sale, shouting we are smashing up the present because we come from the future and cannot run hot and wild without having released the colts. Oh, how we want to have done this with you. To have carried babies inside us to manifold protests and actions and after they come out to have held them fast to us as we eat chicken with the grocery store baggers, our breasts full of milk, letting anyone who wants to suck at them, as the chemicals we produce will provide healthy and complementary amino acids to our feasting, strengthening the immune system for the viruses to come, with or without feelings of comfort or excitability on the giving or receiving ends, and if whether on the giving or on the receiving end of such suckling anyone of us begin to blush from embarrassment, out of fear that such exchanges might be reenacting cliché and problematic tropes of idealized motherhood or the sexualizing of adult nursing or the exploited domestic and reproductive labor of child-rearing women or the gratuitous titillations of public breast-feeding among North Americans, we will pause and wipe our milk moustaches and feeling the heat in our cheeks we shall buck ourselves up, for there is no shame in the free and consensual sharing of resources or in the complicated emotions such sharing can frequently elicit in zones of temporary erogeny. And if some of the milk drips and dribbles onto the ground, splashing in with the dripping cunt-chicken juices and yellow-white blister-pus and tick-bite-nipple discharge, we will not be surprised in the least to find our ranks swelling even further with the plush and the furried, the winged and the clawed, the night-beasts with their quivering snouts leading them to the feast. For look, here among us now, jack-rabbits nibbling on rotten apple cores and red-winged blackbirds falling from the sky and demented panda bears drifting on broken-off ice-shelves, wigged-out cuckoo birds breaking out of vandalized workplace clocks, and mountain lions, leopards, red foxes, kangaroos, feral cats spitting in the night, wild dogs and horses, horses, horses, horses, all holding us upside down so as to hypnotize us and then using the forefinger and middle finger to press down the vent area just in front of our anus so as to make our sex organs protrude, fingering these gently as we write furiously from this position.

And then maybe just then will be heard a dank vibration, halfway between hum and roar, gurgling up from the tangle of nerves that thread round our guts, our first brains brewing in intestinal funk, then up and out the throat, the invisible sound waves resonating between each animal-body, twisting into feedback loops of blistering distortion within and among all the raw mammalian feelers, coursing through the circuits, each meridian charged up with electrified chi. Yes, that just happened, we are materialists who read horoscopes and poets who say chi, freed from constriction and habit, from impasse and defeat, from all that says no inside of us, from all that has been done in our name and still shits out of us, with or without clumps of it sticking in our feathers and fur so that we will never forget, and so that now in the variable buzz of all in consort, tone poems coalescing into tenfold operatics, the fibers of all muscles rippling with the ground tremors of the high-heeled work-booted parade, with leaping and grasping, with or without eye contact, with or without the holding of hands or the light touching of the back or the front, all pressed up against the sweet metallic smell of our entanglement, group-flesh groping ever toward something greater than ourselves, because an army of lovers cannot fail, and with chins up and chests out, bursting forth from the ground into all directions, fists lifted, a thousand middle fingers thrust up in pride and vigor, for all tomorrow's parties today, in heat and in fury, nostrils flaring, each as each can and as each desires, shoulders to it now, leaning ever toward what will have had to have been done to become that which we cannot yet dare envision beyond the sweet taste of it on our moist upper lips—

ACKNOWLEDGMENTS

This has been a three-year project. And it has three years' worth of debts. We will list some of them here. For those we have misplaced or forgotten, we apologize. It has been three years. There have been a lot of drafts.

We began this collaboration by writing "A Picturesque Story About the Border Between Two Cities" for the N 49 15.832 - W 123 05.921 *Positions* Colloquium. Thanks Andrea Actis, Donato Mancini, Nicholas Perrin, and the Kootenay School of Writing collective for the impetus to begin. Thanks to Bhanu Kapil for the names Demented Panda and Koki. Thanks Abby Crain, Bill Luoma, Mark McGurl, Erika Staiti, Charles Weigl, and Stephanie Young for reading drafts and offering feedback. Sections from this book have been previously published (and generously edited by) *Bomb, Lana Turner, Tarpaulin Sky, Floor,* and *Drown My Book: Conceptual Writing By Women.* Previous drafts and other ancillary materials related to the production of this book have appeared in *Cannot Exist* and *Try*.

Charles Bernstein's "The Sixties, With Apologies" is from *Recalculating* (U of Chicago, 2013). Rod Smith's "*Pour le CGT*" was previously printed in *26: A Journal of Poetry and Poetics* (Issue C, 2004). Both are reprinted by permission of the authors.

As we wrote this, we read a lot and we talked about our reading a lot and in parts of this book this reading and discussion shows up but it isn't always clearly marked.

"A Picturesque Story About the Border Between Two Cities" is in part homage to César Aira's *An Episode in the Life of a Landscape Painter* (translated by Chris Andrews). And it quotes or alludes to Vince Neil, Tommy Lee, Mick Mars, and Nikki Sixx, with Neil Strauss's *The Dirt: Confessions of the World's Most Notorious Rock Band*, Livy's *History of Rome*, David Samuels's "Rock is dead: Sex, drugs, and raw sewage at Woodstock 99" (*Harper's*, November 1999), and *Invasive Plants of California's Wildlands*, edited by Carla C. Bossard, John M. Randall, and Marc C. Hoshovsky.

The poem that is quoted in the first "The Side Effect" is Muriel Rukeyser's "Panacea." It is reprinted by permission of International Creative Management,

Inc., copyright © by Muriel Rukeyser. Frank Sherlock, in response to an email we sent out asking for gossip supplied the phrase "ice queen" and this phrase in turn provoked much of this piece. Bob Ostertag's "All the Rage," Cornelius Cardew's *Stockhausen Serves Imperialism*, Matthew Herbert's "Personal Contract for the Composition of Music," Eugene Gendlin's *Focusing*, Tom Wilson's *How to Rebuild Your Volkswagen Air-cooled Engine*, *Free Culture Manifesto*, and Kathy Acker's "Dead Doll Humility" also were influences.

"What We Talk About When We Talk About Poetry" owes an obvious debt to Raymond Carver's "What We Talk About When We Talk About Love" from *What We Talk About When We Talk About Love*, copyright © 1974, 1976, 1978, 1980, 1981 by Raymond Carver. Used by permission of Alfred A. Knopf, a division of Random House Inc. Any third-party use of this material, outside of this publication, is prohibited. Interested parties must apply directly to Random House Inc. for permission. Mark Scroggins's *The Poem of a Life: A Biography of Louis Zukofsky* and Tim Woods's *The Poetics of the Limit: Ethics and Politics in Modern and Contemporary American Poetry* shaped our thinking. We also are indebted to some comments made by Louis Cabri on Zukofsky's "'A'-9" at the 95 cent skool in the summer of 2010 and some generous emails from Michael Cross.

The poem that is quoted in the second "The Side Effect" is William Wordsworth's "Daffodils." We also drew from Melanie Klein's "The Psychogenesis of Manic-Depressive States" and the Abu Ghraib photographs. CAConrad twice wrote (Soma)tic Exercises for us. The soup scene and the piece that is read to the dogs in "The Side Effect" are the products of these exercises. These exercises are collected in his *A Beautiful Marsupial Afternoon: New (Soma)tics*. We hope you get this book and make your own soup.

"Army of Lovers" is so full of reference that we probably couldn't re-create a complete bibliography for it. Some obvious sources include Ronald Havens's and Catherine Walter's *Hypnotherapy Scripts: A Neo-Eriksonian Approach to Persuasive Healing*, Gendlin's *Focusing*, Silvia Federici's *Caliban and the Witch*, the VOINA group, William Pope.L, Deborah Hay, Frank O'Hara's "Personism: A Manifesto," and various websites on mutualism and the like. The title was inspired by a painting by Ginger Brooks Takahashi.

David Buuck lives in Oakland, CA. He is the founder of BARGE, the Bay Area Research Group in Enviro-aesthetics, and co-founder and editor of *Tripwire*, a journal of poetics. Books include *The Shunt* (Palm Press, 2009) and *SITE CITE CITY* (Futurepoem, 2014).

Juliana Spahr lives in Berkeley, CA. She is the author of four books of poetry: *Well Then There Now* (Black Sparrow, 2011), *This Connection of Everyone with Lungs* (UC Press, 2005), *Fuck You-Aloha-I Love You* (Wesleyan, 2001), and *Response* (Sun & Moon, 1996). In 2007 she published *The Transformation* (Atelos), a book of prose. She edits with Jena Osman the book series Chain Links and with nineteen other poets the collectively funded Subpress. She has edited numerous critical anthologies and teaches at Mills College.

Photo © Andrew Kenower